THE EHRICH WEISZ CHRONICLES

DEMON GATE

To Lorna

Nothing is as it seems!

THE EHRICH WEISZ CHRONICLES

DEMON GATE

MARTY CHAN

Fitzhenry & Whiteside

Published in Canada by Fitzhenry & Whiteside,
195 Allstate Parkway, Markham, Ontario L3R 4T8

Published in the United States in 2013 by Fitzhenry & Whiteside,
311 Washington Street, Brighton, Massachusetts 02135

www.fitzhenry.ca godwit@fitzhenry.ca

10 9 8 7 6 5 4 3 2 1

Library and Archives Canada Cataloguing in Publication
Chan, Marty, author
The Ehrich Weisz chronicles : demon gate / Marty Chan.
ISBN 978-1-55455-306-8 (pbk.)
I. Title.
PS8555.H39244E47 2013 jC813'.54 C2013-906404-4

Publisher Cataloging-in-Publication Data (U.S.)
The Ehrich Weisz Chronicles: Demon Gate
ISBN 978-1-55455-306-8 (Paperback)
Data available on file

Fitzhenry & Whiteside acknowledges with thanks the Canada Council for the Arts, and the Ontario Arts Council for their support of our publishing program. We acknowledge the financial support of the Government of Canada through the Canada Book Fund (CBF) for our publishing activities.

Canada Council for the Arts Conseil des arts du Canada

Cover design by Tanya Montini
Text design by Daniel Choi
Cover image courtesy of Shutterstock | Cover art courtesy of Suzanne Del Rizzo
Printed in Canada by Friesens

ACKNOWLEDGEMENTS

A hearty round of applause to the Alberta Foundation for the Arts, Canada Council for the Arts, and Edmonton Public Library for the support of my first draft. Bravo to the Edmowrimos for the word wars that helped me write a zero draft. And a standing ovation to the kind people who pointed the way to the finish line. Thanks to Christie Harkin, Brad Smilanich, Wei Wong, Stephen Tsang, Tanya Montini, Daniel Choi, Suzanne Del Rizzo, Tom Meyers, Greg Young, and the library staff at the New-York Historical Society.

For Michelle and Ben

From Nov. 1, 1926 *Detroit Record*

MAGICIAN TAKES SECRETS TO GRAVE

Detroit, Nov. 1 – Harry Houdini's mysterious feats of escape, which thrilled spectators throughout his illustrious career, today were overshadowed by the mystery of his untimely death. He passed away at Detroit's Grace Hospital last night, taking with him the secrets of how he escaped from manacles, chains, coffins, straitjackets and other contrivances.

Although Houdini wrote copiously on magic, his own methods were never revealed, nor have they ever been duplicated by any of his contemporaries, thus setting him apart as the world's greatest magician. Later in life, he gained a reputation for exposing charlatans posing as mediums, which earned him a few detractors in the world of spiritualism.

Houdini is believed to have perished as a result of a ruptured appendix, but the exact circumstances of Houdini's death are currently unknown.

AN UNEXPECTED ENTRY

Any other time he could spring a lock, but this one refused to open. Maybe the dim lighting in the unfamiliar hallway made it hard to see. Perhaps the sweat on his hands caused his hook pick to shift and prevented the lock pins from lifting. Maybe he was crumbling under the pressure of his first live performance in front of his kid brother. Whatever the reason, Ehrich Weisz could not still the tension wrench in his trembling hand.

"We should leave," Dash whispered, nervously scratching under the waistband of his knickerbockers.

"Just keep watch," Ehrich said. A Hungarian accent clung to his speech like caked mud on the side of a boot, not yet ready to fall off.

"We don't need to do this. I can tell Momma my cap fell in the river."

"Dash, you know her. She will wonder why we were near the

Fox in the first place. Besides, if you let Gregor take your hat today, he is going to take something else from you tomorrow."

The ten-year-old boy's thick eyebrows furrowed like the wings of a crow in mid-flight. "Why do you not tell him to give it back?"

In 1888 America, one did not get anything by asking; instead, you had to take what you wanted. The problem was that Gregor had four years on the twelve-year-old Ehrich; plus, he outweighed both Weisz brothers combined. If Ehrich could challenge him to a tumbling contest, maybe he'd have a chance, but flying fists beat backflips every time. The solution was to take something Gregor cared about—something Ehrich could offer as a trade—and he knew what to steal: Gregor's prized clay marbles. The German teen had amassed quite the collection over the last year, mostly by intimidating weak-kneed players into forfeiting their marbles. The games reminded Ehrich how the husky boy dominated the neighbourhood. Every kid was a marble, and it was only a matter of time before Gregor knocked him out of the circle. Dash had bested the bully, and the enraged teen accused his brother of cheating, then confiscated his hat.

Ehrich wiped his sweaty cheek against the shoulder of his sack jacket and redoubled his efforts on the lock. The hook pick slid deeper as a pin lifted. A bead of sweat rolled down his anchor-like nose as he turned the tension wrench. *Click!*

"I'm in," he whispered, barely able to disguise his glee.

But he wasn't the one who opened the door. A burly man with more hair than flesh stood in the doorway, his rotund belly spilling over the waistband of his wool trousers.

"Who are you?" Gregor's father bellowed.

Ehrich shoved his brother back down the hall. "Run!"

"Damn kids. Come back here!"

The Weisz brothers scrambled down the steps and burst out of the apartment building. Ehrich sprinted ahead along the wooden sidewalk, ducking between well-groomed men in frocks and coifed women in Dolman cloaks.

"Wait! Wait for me!" Dash screamed.

Ehrich grabbed his brother's arm and yanked him around the corner. The heavyset man shouted, "Little brats! I'll tan your hides until you can't sit for a week!"

Ehrich dodged oncoming horse carriages to cross the wide muddy road. Dash gasped for air, unable to run any further.

"Hide!" Ehrich ordered.

"What about you?"

"Whatever you do, do not come out until I find you." He shoved his little brother behind a pile of trash and then sprinted in the opposite direction, drawing Gregor's father after him.

The angry man barrelled right past Dash. The young boy wiped the sweat from his bushy eyebrows as he searched for a better, less smelly, hiding place. Halfway down the block, a narrow alleyway seemed a likely sanctuary. Dash scanned the area for Nosy Nellies. None of the crowd cared about him; they were more interested in the chase. He ducked into the alley and threaded past barrels and crates. A man's leg twitched on the other side of a wooden box. Dash stiffened.

"Is anybody there? Hello?"

A man with a golden handlebar moustache sat against the brick wall, his head listing. His twitching foot repeatedly kicked the wooden crate. Sulphur lingered in the air.

"Are you all right, sir?" Dash asked, covering his nose.

The man lifted his head. Only the whites of his eyes gazed out.

The stench of sulphur grew stronger. Soft hands grabbed Dash from behind. He opened his mouth to scream, but nothing came out.

Ehrich yelped. Gregor's father had a firm grip of his ear. "Where's the other brat?"

"Ow! Let go! Ow!"

"Not until I find a copper."

A thrashing, Ehrich could handle, but jail time? No way. His parents would be furious.

"Help!" he cried out. "He's trying to kidnap me!"

The husky man stiffened and loosened his grip as he noticed the boy's conniption fit had attracted curious bystanders. This distraction was all Ehrich needed to slip out of the man's meaty grasp and bolt across the street. He vaulted over a hitching post. Gregor's father continued the chase, but he took a wide berth around a crowd of stern men deciding whether or not to act. Ehrich rounded a corner and slammed into a rain barrel, almost winding himself. His pursuer sounded like he was almost upon him.

No time to think, Ehrich doffed his cap, climbed into the half-full barrel and dunked his entire body in the cold water. He contorted himself into a tight ball so that he was entirely submerged. A strong swimmer, he could hold his breath, but not indefinitely. He heard the distorted echo of approaching footsteps on the wooden sidewalk. They stopped near him. Silence.

Ehrich puffed his cheeks, forcing his lungs to use the little oxygen he had left. His neck strained and his chest burned.

Had Gregor's father discovered him? He counted to distract himself from the pain. "One... two... three... four..." He mentally screamed, "Land sakes! Keep walking! No one here. Eight... nine... ten... elev—"

Finally, the footsteps moved away. Ehrich shot out of the water, gasping. He peered over the rain barrel's rim. No sign of Gregor's father. He climbed out as a prim woman in a Zouave jacket scurried past and stared. Ever the showman, Ehrich swept his soaking cap back with a flourish as he took a bow. The dark-haired lady huffed in disdain. Grinning, Ehrich set off in search of Dash.

Ehrich jogged briskly, leaving a trail of water behind him. A flicker of movement to the left—the younger Weisz was scurrying down a street, heading away from the crowds.

"Dash?"

The boy didn't respond.

"Dash! Where are you going?"

Nothing. Was his brother mad at him for leaving him alone? Was he going home to tell their mother? Ehrich quickened his pace but slowed when Dash headed to the outskirts of town. He followed until he recognized their destination—the cemetery. Here in this desolate field, the only life was a few scraggly elms clinging to the last of their sparse autumn covering.

Ehrich started after his brother, but stopped when he heard footsteps pounding behind him. Had Gregor's father caught up? He couldn't take the chance and veered off to the right to misdirect the unseen pursuer. He angled away from the cemetery and back toward the buildings, picking up the pace as he ducked into an alley. He glanced back and saw no one. Maybe his imagination had played tricks on him. He started to move, but froze when he saw Gregor's father turn the corner. Ehrich ducked behind a pile of boxes and inched away, slipping deeper into the neighbourhood. He navigated a maze of streets and stopped at the corner of an apartment building. He waited for a few minutes until he was sure he'd given Gregor's father the slip, then he returned to the graveyard.

Ehrich reached the edge of the cemetery and heard a low hum. He moved past the grave markers toward the source until he saw his brother. In the middle of the graveyard, Dash had set up a bizarre contraption that looked like the skeletal frame of a tepee without the buffalo hide. A Medusa's head of wires sprouted from a large copper box at the base of the pole. Azure tendrils of plasma energy lazily swirled around the cylinder and rotor blades spun until they were perpendicular to the ground. The loud whine grew louder until Ehrich had to cover his ears.

A slit appeared in the heart of the tube. The glowing opening widened slowly like a cat's eye.

To Ehrich's astonishment, the horizon of a blood red sky dawned in the newly formed gateway. Giant sentinels in iron armour lined the parapets of a walled city. Brass gate doors loomed in the foreground. Dash stood up and stepped toward the shimmering portal.

Ehrich finally found his voice. "Dash! What are you doing?"

The whirring blades drowned him out. He ran across the cemetery and tackled Dash before his brother could step through. They fell to the ground in an explosion of autumn leaves. Ehrich rolled against the base of the machine and jarred it. New images appeared in the gateway.

Dash scrambled across the ground and head-butted his big brother, knocking him away from the contraption. Dazed, the older Weisz tried to stand, but a swift foot caught him in the midsection, sending him rolling across the grass until his back slammed against a wooden grave marker. *Crack*!

Dash knelt over the control box. Ehrich scrambled to his feet and tackled the small boy, throwing him off balance. They both flew into the maw of the rift in space. Ehrich's brain seemed to separate from his skull. He couldn't tell if he was falling or standing; instead, he felt as if he was floating in the ocean and plummeting from a tree at the same time. A kaleidoscope of images rushed past him: a building that hung from the bottom of a cloud, a beach where a fish wobbled on hairy legs, a giant bronze torch in the hands of the massive statue of a woman.

Then, just as suddenly as they appeared, the images were gone and Ehrich slammed into the device's centre pole, toppling it. He skidded across a cobblestone street with Dash on top of his chest. The rotors sliced into the uneven ground, shattering against the stone; one of the shards missing Ehrich's head by inches. As Dash rose to his feet, Ehrich clutched frantically at the front of his brother's shirt, tearing at the collar, but a body slammed into his back, knocking him to the ground.

Shouts of angry Irish fighters rang in the air, punctuated with screams of pain. They were clearly in the middle of a Five-Points donnybrook. Ehrich spotted at least three bodies lying in the mud with knife wounds. Around him, tenement buildings blocked out the light and what little sky that was left had been blotted out by black smoke.

Dash wrenched himself out of his brother's grasp and ran into the melee. Ehrich tried to climb to his feet, but his legs wobbled. When he found his balance, he spotted the younger boy sprinting across the street toward the outer ring of fighters where a man with mutton-chop sideburns and a bloodied white shirt brandished a wicked knife at another man with a torn white undershirt. As Dash glanced behind him, he unwittingly stepped between the combatants and into the path of the thrusting blade. Too late, the two fighters reeled back as Dash lurched to a sudden stop. The small boy clutched the blade in his gut and staggered two steps before he collapsed.

"Dash! No!" Ehrich stepped dazedly onto the street as two black stallions pulling an oncoming coach reared up, one of them clipping Ehrich's temple and sending him sprawling across the road. As he was losing consciousness, he witnessed the carriage careen over. Then he passed out.

When he came to, the fighting had stopped. Amid the groans of the survivors, comrades dragged the bloody bodies of their fallen friends away. Ehrich sat up groggily and scanned the square for Dash but found no sign of him. He felt something pressing into his palm—a shred of his brother's shirt and a medallion hooked on a broken leather strap.

Two gear wheels soldered together to form a figure-eight. Inside the twin loops, smaller gears connected to each other, getting smaller and smaller as if they could extend to infinity. An image of a lion with the head of a goat on its shoulders and a snake for a tail was engraved on the medallion's back cover. What the Chimera meant, where Dash had gotten this strange medallion from, and why he had been wearing it around his neck, Ehrich had no idea.

MR. SANDMAN STRIKES

Sleep was the young boy's enemy. He refused to lie down, despite his mother's best efforts.

"Mother, something comes at night. I don't know what it is, but I think it wants to hurt me," he whispered.

"Such an imagination." She tousled the boy's curly blond locks. "Aren't you tuckered out yet?"

"I'm sure there's a creature in my room." He stared at the lacquered cabinet in the corner. The gilded design resembled snakes climbing to the top. "Sometimes, I hear it knocking."

She drew the soft cotton quilt up to his chin. "That's the house settling."

"No, the monster lives in the cabinet. It wants to eat me."

"Shh, shh, time to sleep." She turned down the oil reservoir valve on the astral lamp, but he grabbed her wrist.

"Please leave the light on," he begged.

She caressed his chubby cheek. "You know what you need?

A bedtime story."

He burrowed the back of his head into the pillow. "Yes! Read me a little more from that book. *The Prince and the Pauper*."

"The book's downstairs. Why don't I tell you a tale about a man who guides children to a magical realm where dreams come true?"

"Who is he?"

"Mr. Sandman. You can tell it's him by his bag of sleeping dust. He blows the fine bits of dust into children's eyes to make their eyelids heavy, and when they fall asleep, he transports them to a train which travels on moonbeam tracks all the way to Slumber."

"Do you think he's in the cabinet?" The boy began to sit up.

She pressed him back to the pillow. "No, but he's on his way. If you're asleep when he comes, he'll put you in the car near the front of the train."

He nestled into the bed.

"Please, leave the lamp on so Mr. Sandman can find me."

She sighed and adjusted the valve to brighten the room just a bit. Then she kissed her son's forehead and walked out. She stopped at the doorway. "Good ni—"

A slight, high-pitched whistle cut her off. In the hallway, a tall man in a raggedy black suit stood a few feet away. Under his stovetop hat, his mottled face resembled a calico cat's colouring. The whistling came from his sickle-shaped nose as he sucked in air.

"Who are you?" she asked, bristling. "What do you want?"

He raised a metal claw-like hand to his lips and blew dust into her eyes.

In the bedroom, the cherubic boy watched in horror as his mother slumped to the floor. Standing over her, the raggedy man in the tattered suit bent over her face and plucked a small orb. He deposited the bloody ball into the satchel at his hip then he touched the woman's face again.

"M-m-mother," the boy stammered.

Her body jerked in the hallway as the creature looked up and ogled the boy, his dappled face illuminated by the bedside lamp's dim light. He flashed a crooked smile, his yellow teeth stalagmites in a fetid cave.

"M-M-Mister Sandman?"

"No, fles-s-sh bag," the raggedy man said, his sibilant speech scratching at the boy's ears. "Ole Lukoje won't be here long. All I want is-s-s your tas-s-sty peepers-s-s."

He hopped over the threshold like a black-billed magpie and curled the fingers of his metal gloves. The overlapping plates of steel were laid like an armadillo's armour while the fingertips were honed to razor-sharp talons.

"I'll go to sleep. I promise. I'll go to sleep," the boy pleaded, shutting his eyes.

Ole Lukoje perched on the foot of the bed, reached into his jacket pocket and drew out some dust. He held his hand to his mouth and prepared to blow.

"I wouldn't do that," a voice said behind him.

A stocky teenager in a tan leather duster tipped a salute with his black bowler, revealing a set of gauges around the hatband. The teen's eyes glinted behind tinted goggles. He aimed a teslatron rifle at the raggedy man's sickle nose. At the end of the barrel that blossomed into a large doughnut-shaped coil, the blunderbuss-styled musket crackled with a blue-white energy.

"Back away from the boy."

Ole Lukoje hopped off the bed.

"Ah, yes-s-s. You mus-s-t want my papers-s-s." He rummaged in his satchel, but produced nothing. "Deares-s-s-t me, I can't s-s-seem to find them."

"How did you get here?" the teen asked.

The raggedy man cocked his head to the side. "I came here like all the other travellers-s-s. Through Demon Gate."

"You're an illegal. Thought you were a burglar at first, but no human thief steals eyes."

Ole Lukoje cracked a thin-lipped smile. "Ah. Yes-s-s, I think I found what I need."

"Stop there." The teen raised his weapon. "Hands out. Put the bag on the floor."

The man in the tattered suit obeyed, dropping his satchel. He kicked it across the floor, spilling out some of the contents. Then he backed toward the window.

"Don't move," the teen ordered. "I said, don't move."

The goggled saviour strode forward. *Squish.* He lifted his heavy black boot. Something sticky and stringy clung to the sole. Ole Lukoje vaulted onto the young man's shoulders and his taloned gloves tore through his duster and thick wool shirt. Both fell to the floor. The teslatron slid under the cabinet. The raggedy man flicked dust into the teen's face, but the particles pinged harmlessly off the tinted goggles. The teen bucked off his attacker, rolled to his feet, and whipped his duster open to draw a volt pistol from his holster. A pencil-thick cylinder flew out the end of the sleek barrel. Ole Lukoje ducked out of the way. An electro-dart cracked the window and a web of electricity dissipated against the non-conductive glass.

The raggedy man swept the lamp from the nightstand and hurled himself out of the window. The cherubic boy, meanwhile, sat bolt upright on the bed, screeching. The teen tried to calm him, but his bug-eyed goggles sent the boy further into a panic. He ripped the goggles off to reveal an anchor-like nose and bushy eyebrows.

"Easy, kid. My name's Ehrich Weisz," he said with barely a trace of his former accent.

"Get away from me! Monster! Monster!"

Ehrich ignored the screaming as he ran his hand through his mop of brown hair. He jumped to the window, but the raggedy man was already halfway down the street. Ehrich hurriedly checked his wounds as he crossed the bedroom. Ole Lukoje's talons had dug deep enough to draw blood, but not enough to slow him down. He holstered his volt pistol and picked up his teslatron. The coil sat askew on the barrel. He cursed the delicate design of the weapon, then pulled his goggles over his eyes and flipped the green filters over the primary lenses. Night turned as bright as day. He left the screaming boy, stepped over the fallen mother, and rushed outside. The hunt was on.

THE HUNTER'S TRAIL

Posh mansions and apartment buildings with intricate stonework bracketed the wide cobblestone road, but Fifth Avenue did not dazzle Ehrich; not when he had his gaze set on tracking his quarry, which he had first spotted, while on patrol, casing the mansion with the mother and her son. The raggedy man was nowhere in sight. Ehrich tracked south in the hopes of spotting some sign of the killer. He lingered outside another mansion, eyeing the light in the upper floor window. A woman stepped in front and pulled the curtains closed, but not before she shot a suspicious glance at Ehrich. None of the wealthy inhabitants had any idea that a deadly stalker was in their midst. He suspected they were more concerned about commoners like himself traipsing past their manicured lawns.

Though he had spent two years in New York, he still couldn't adjust to this dimension's city. Technological advancements in weapons such as his volt pistol and teslatron rifle were a marvel. So were the steam-powered generators that heated the warehouses in Fulton market. The dirigible moored on the Statue of Liberty's raised torch still gave him pause, but some things did not change.

"Get your evening news. All that's fit to print," a young girl in a dirty grey smock yelled out. She eyed Ehrich. "You want a paper?"

He fished two pennies from his pocket and held them out. When she reached for them, he closed his fist. "I don't want yesterday's news. I want to know what's happening now."

The girl wiped her sleeve against her lips, never taking her gaze off his hand. "That'll cost you extra."

He smirked. The girl reminded him of the year he had spent on the streets hawking newspapers to make enough money to buy a cooked yam or a bag of roasted peanuts, his only meal on some days. To survive in the Bowery, you needed to know how to take advantage of whatever opportunity sprang up, and this girl smelled opportunity.

Ehrich reached into his pocket and fished out three more pennies. The girl's eyes twinkled as she stared at the coins on the palm of his hand. He closed his hand before the guttersnipe could even think about snatching the pennies.

"You know they tell me not to talk to Demon Watch hunters," she said. "I'm taking a big risk here. Should be worth more than what you've got there."

"Bully for you, but this is all you're going to get," Ehrich said. "I'm sure I can find a hungrier newsie down the street."

"No, no, I'll take it." She opened her hand.

Ehrich had survived long enough in the Bowery to avoid this trick. "Not until you tell me what you know."

"But if I tell you, then you have no reason to pay me."

"You're going to have to trust me," he said.

"They say we're not supposed to trust your kind. Heard you grab kids like me off the street and make 'em work in Demon Gate over on Devil's Island."

"Sure," he said. "Demon Watch is always on the lookout for strays. That dimensional portal doesn't run itself." One thing Ehrich had learned in his time in New York was how to manipulate someone's assumptions to his advantage. "If you don't give me what I want right quick, I can haul you back with me so you can work with the worst of the worst. The ones down in the prisons. Think the Dimensionals out here are bad? Tip of the iceberg."

The guttersnipe's eyes widened. "You wouldn't...would you?"

The truth was Demon Watch did recruit orphans, but they found more skilled and better-motivated trainees from orphanages than on the streets. This girl couldn't even cut kitchen duty, let alone a shift in Demon Gate. On the other hand, Ehrich had proven his mettle early on and graduated from cleaning dormitories to hunter training within a few months. By the looks of this stick of a girl, she'd be turned back to the streets before she could say her name. Of course, she didn't need to know that.

"Yep, you'd be perfect for Demon Gate. Get you nice and close to the new arrivals. Some of them can be nasty. So, do we have a deal?"

She nodded.

"Good. I'm looking for a man in a black tattered suit. Curved nose like a hook. Went running past here a minute ago."

Trembling, the girl pointed along the road leading toward

the heart of the Bowery. Ehrich grimaced. His old stomping grounds. He grabbed the girl's hand.

"You promised you wouldn't..." she wailed.

He dropped the coins into her hand then set off after the raggedy man. Soon, the gated mansions were gone, replaced by the seedy tenements that blocked out the sky. The Bowery teemed with night owls peddling their wares under dangling telephone wires, hanging shop signs and colourful awnings. Thick Irish accents competed with guttural German and Italian as merchants bandied back and forth with customers. Ehrich winced at the stench of dead oysters and stale potatoes. He passed a couple of dark-skinned women hawking corn from their pushcarts.

"Corn for sale. Sweet, sweet corn for sale," one sang, beckoning him with her skinny ebony finger.

"Not interested."

"You need to eat some—" She stopped when his duster flapped open to reveal his weapon.

She backed away, singing to another potential customer. The street teemed with people but none of them were his prey.

"Anyone come across a tall man in a raggedy black suit?" he asked.

No one answered. Bowery denizens did not talk to figures of authority like coppers or Demon Watch hunters. His volt pistol and goggles gave him away. He pulled his tan duster closed to hide the weapon. As much as they hated Dimensionals, this collection of merchants, scam artists and hoodlums hated Demon Watch even more. No one was going to talk to him.

Dirty-faced men in shoddy outdated sack jackets stumbled along stone sidewalks to find the nearest tavern. A street urchin squeezed between the men and snatched a hot cob of corn from a cart. The vendor nabbed him by the ear.

Then an unearthly shriek shattered the night air. Ehrich sprinted to the end of the block and veered into a narrow street. Even in the dark, he recognized this place—Bandit's Roost, an alley where thieves and murderers lurked. He drew his pistol and flicked the switch on the side of his bowler hat. A faint glow chased the shadows away. Drying clothes hung on overhead lines strung between the brick tenements. The uneven cobblestones echoed under Ehrich's boots as he crept past barrels and porches. To the right, he noticed a stairwell leading down, most likely to a gambling den. Crates and garbage littered the alley. He stepped over the debris, expecting someone to jump out from the darkened doorways on either side of him.

A bright glow lit the end of the road. Ehrich hurried toward it until he reached the sliver of a shimmering portal hanging in the air. The gateway slowly expanded while the raggedy man hopped over a female corpse, waiting for the portal to grow wider.

"Turn around," Ehrich barked, raising his weapon.

Ole Lukoje hissed.

"Come toward me. Slowly."

The raggedy man glanced back at the portal, but it was too narrow. He slid his hands into his jacket pockets.

"No, no. Hands where I can see them this time."

He obeyed, but as his hands rose, dust poured from his fists. The cascading stream landed on the corpse, and her body began to twitch. The woman sat up, her bloody throat ripped open and her empty eye sockets glowing a deep blue. The front of her tattered, grey, cotton shirt was stained with blood. She rose to her feet and grabbed a metal pipe from the garbage pile next to her.

Ehrich aimed his volt pistol at Ole Lukoje, but the reanimated woman blocked the shot. Every time he adjusted his aim, she jumped in the way.

"Move!"

The raggedy man let out a sickly cackle. "The dead won't obey you."

"I said *move*." He fired, but the woman batted the dart away. It struck the brick wall behind her, erupting into a blast of electricity. The dust had endowed her corpse with unnatural speed and strength.

The portal now was wide enough for the raggedy man to slip through. Ehrich threw himself to the side of the alley and fired high over the woman's head at the portal. Branches of electricity lit up the gateway like an oil-soaked rag catching a flame just as Ole Lukoje reached his hand into the opening.

The portal instantly closed in on the raggedy man's arm. He shrieked as the gateway sealed up, lopping off his arm just below the elbow.

Meanwhile, the reanimated woman lurched toward Ehrich who managed to squeeze off one more shot as she swung the pipe at his hand. The electro-dart flew wide and struck the frame of an opened window. Energy danced across the lace curtains, sparking into flame.

Pain shot up Ehrich's arm and he dropped the weapon. He slammed his other hand into the woman's solar plexus, but it had no effect. She swung the pipe at his head, forcing him to duck. Ehrich spun away before she could swing again. He stumbled into a busy thoroughfare, crowded with late-night patrons leaving a local rum hole. The sight of the woman's bloody throat and glowing eyes halted their drunken hijinks, allowing the frazzled Weisz to slip between them and escape.

The harsh glow of arc lamps on Houston Street was a welcome sight. He scrambled away while the reanimated woman chased after him. The loud crackle of a nearby arc lamp startled her, and she gave the lamp a wide berth.

Ah ha, thought Ehrich. She has a weakness.

He sprinted to the next lamppost, hoisted himself up the thick pole and shimmied up. He was about halfway to the top when a shrill whistle pierced the night. The woman cocked her head like a curious bird, then cawed. The raggedy man approached, looking like the Grim Reaper himself, clutching the cauterized nub of his right arm. The muscular Weisz tried to climb higher, but his grip slipped and he slid down the post where his pursuer was waiting for him. He landed awkwardly on his left ankle, and grabbed the post to steady himself.

Before Ehrich could get to his feet, the woman caught him under the chin with her pipe and pressed it against his throat, pinning him against the post. He struggled to break free, but the undead woman was too strong. Stars began to dance before his eyes.

Ehrich tried to shove the woman away, but she didn't budge. Her glowing eye sockets flared brighter and the gash across her throat looked like a cruel smile.

Ole Lukoje hissed, "S-s-stop."

The pressure eased slightly off his throat.

"The pleasure of extinguish-s-shing this fles-s-sh bag's-s-s life will be mine," the raggedy man said.

"You're under arrest," Ehrich gasped.

The mottled-faced Dimensional giggled. "Empty threats-s-s from a dying boy."

Ehrich kicked the poor woman in the mid-section, but she didn't even flinch.

"Hey, ugly! Over here," a voice interrupted. Ole Lukoje whirled around to see a blond-haired boy in a tan duster aiming a teslatron rifle at his chest.

"Charlie!" Ehrich gasped. "Watch out for his dust!"

The eighteen-year-old kept his weapon aimed at Ole Lukoje. "Thanks for the warning. Margaret, Louis—let's bag him."

Charlie advanced, herding the raggedy man to the right, where two other hunters were waiting. They rushed behind Ole Lukoje and tossed a net over him. Ole Lukoje struggled to break free from the wire mesh while Margaret pinned him.

The reanimated woman yanked her pipe from Ehrich's throat and ran to save her master, leaving Ehrich dazed and gasping for air. Louis tried to draw his volt pistol, but before he could aim, she swung the pipe and knocked the weapon out of his hand—then she speared Louis in the gut with its sharp butt-end. His hiccupping gasps sent chills down Ehrich's spine.

Ehrich dove for the pistol and shot into the reanimated woman's exposed back. Her body twitched as the energy coursed through her system. Points of light exploded under the skin of her face and her glowing eye sockets flared a bright blue before fading out. Whatever power controlled the corpse was destroyed, and her limp, broken body crumpled to the cobblestone street. Ehrich rushed to Louis, who lay clutching the pipe imbedded in his stomach. Blood pooled across his shirt.

A shrill whistle pierced Ehrich's ears. He turned to see the raggedy man, still under the net, rolling on top of Margaret. A moment later, Charlie managed to slam the butt of his teslatron into the back of Ole Lukoje's head, knocking him out.

Charlie pulled the goggles from his face and nodded at Ehrich. "How's Louis?"

He shook his head. His friend ran a hand through his dirty blond hair and took a breath. Behind him, two new hunters—Gino and Wilhelm—rushed up.

The lanky Wilhelm panted, "Crowd held us up. We got here as fast as we could. What happened?"

"Help Margaret wrap up the illegal," said Charlie.

Gino snapped to attention. "Yes, sir."

"On it," Wilhelm said.

"Ehrich, give me a hand with Louis."

"Yes, lieutenant." Ehrich answered, knowing better than to show too much familiarity with the squad leader of the Demon Watch hunters, even if Charlie Campbell was his best friend.

Suddenly, a voice cried out, "Bandit's Roost is burning!" Hawkers left their pushcarts and rushed toward an orange glow down the street. The night sky was lit up over the Bowery.

Ehrich's throat closed as he recalled the electro-dart sparking against the curtains. He turned to his friend. "Charlie, we have to help them."

The team leader shook his head. "No, we have to get Louis to the surgeon. A fire in the slums is the least of our worries."

Ehrich took one last look at the orange glow, hoping he wasn't the cause. But the sinking feeling in his stomach told him he knew the truth.

SEARCH FOR A SCAPEGOAT

Normally, George Farrier enjoyed the newspaper. It was his one respite against the overwhelmingly tedious routine of running Demon Gate. He appreciated reading about the daily events of New York, even the odd grisly murder, because the stories transported him away from the daily grind of the facility.

Today, however, the front-page story brought him right back to Devil's Island.

The newspaper headline read: *Bowery Blaze*. Accompanying the article was a cartoonist's illustration of a Demon Watch hunter dancing in front of a blazing tenement. He lowered the broadsheet, rested his elbows on his oak-top desk, and sighed at the fresh-faced teenagers standing at full attention the entire time he had been re-reading the article. Their dingy dusters seemed out of place in this opulent setting of antique furniture and exotic trinkets.

Some people collected coins. Others collected art. Farrier

collected souvenirs from the Dimensionals who came to New York. The array of items on a nearby rosewood table ranged from a necklace of serrated teeth to a colourful egg with animated images scrolling across the surface. On the far side of the roomy office, an Oriental cabinet bore more trinkets: a golden orb with mechanical wings, a mantle clock with glowing green numbers, and a brass spider clutching red silk between its mandibles.

The barrel-chested commander leaned forward in a leather chair that creaked under his weight, and he placed his ham-hock hands on the newsprint, showing off the scars running up the length of both arms. Farrier's salt and pepper beard gave his face some grace, but there was no hiding the scars across the bridge of his nose and over his left eye. A Civil War veteran, he wore his wounds like medals.

Farrier's gaze took in Ehrich's torn duster, then moved on to Charlie and the three other surviving members of the squad: the snub-nosed bruiser, Margaret, who had helped capture Ole Lukoje; the rake-thin whiner, Wilhelm; and the lazy-eyed joker, Gino. Only Louis was absent; he lay in the infirmary, fighting for his life.

"Who started the fire in Bandit's Roost?" he asked the five teens.

Charlie stiffened. "Sir, I don't know what you're talking about."

Farrier shook his head. "Tarnation! No games. I want to know who started the fire in the Bowery. Immediately."

"No one we would know of, sir. None of my hunters were in Bandit's Roost."

Ehrich cast a sideways glance at Margaret and Wilhelm, but they stared straight ahead, refusing to contradict their squad leader. Gino's lazy eye wandered to Charlie.

"We patrolled Fifth Avenue when we made first contact," their squad leader recounted. "We followed the creature to the Bowery. We didn't go anywhere near Bandit's Roost."

Farrier drummed his fingers on his desk. "Really? That's your story?"

"Yes, commander," Charlie answered.

The old man turned to the others. "Do you concur?"

Margaret and Gino nodded. Wilhelm snapped to attention. "Yes, sir."

Ehrich stared straight ahead, but he could sense Farrier watching him.

"Mr. Weisz, do you concur?"

Ehrich hesitated.

Charlie came to the rescue. "He does."

"I'd like to hear from Mr. Weisz."

"Sir, we caught an illegal and shut down his portal. We did our job," Ehrich said. He wasn't about to let Farrier push him around, even if he was the head of Demon Watch.

Farrier narrowed his gaze. "Were you or were you not near Bandit's Roost?"

"No."

The commander cocked his head to one side. "Are you certain?"

"Yes, sir."

"Then help me reconcile the fact that the police found an electro-dart in one of the burned-out buildings. Your squad was the only one in the area at the time of the fire. Furthermore, five witnesses reported seeing a hunter matching your description, Mr. Weisz, firing this dart through a window."

“The people in Bandit’s Roost are thieves and murderers,” Ehrich said. “Lying wouldn’t be that much of a stretch.”

“Didn’t we recruit you from that area?”

Ehrich fell silent.

Farrier held up the newspaper. “The mayor’s office has been swamped with complaints about the Bowery episode. He’s even worried the *World* may send Nellie Bly to write an exposé like the one she did on Blackwell’s Island.”

“They say any press is good press,” Gino said.

Margaret and Wilhelm elbowed their comrade in the ribs to shut him up.

“If the people saw what the demon did to the boy’s mother, they’d be down on their knees thanking us,” Charlie insisted. “She’s lucky that creature only took her eyes and not her life.”

“Tarnation. So much like Nicholas...” Farrier mumbled, shaking his head.

“Sir?”

The bearded commander stood up and limped to the window behind his desk. His peg leg was another memento of the Civil War. He placed his hands behind his back and stared out at the grave markers littering the field. His silence weighed heavily on the hunters, forcing their shoulders to sag.

After several moments, Farrier spoke, his voice low. “I’ve dug my share of graves. One for my best friend. Two for my brothers. Seventeen for my fellow soldiers. Some of them just knee high to a cricket... the damn war.”

This dimension’s Civil War was one of the bloodiest in the country’s history and had resulted in the fundamental difference between the two worlds Ehrich straddled. During the battles, inter-dimensional gateways had opened up and allowed a stream of Dimensionals to descend on America. Some of the early beings' grotesque appearances inspired the offensive nickname they had been given—demons. Soon, fear of an invasion gripped the nation. Soldiers set aside their allegiances to the North or South and banded together to put down the demons. The hunt took many years and cost countless humans and Dimensionals their lives.

Farrier stepped away from the window, limped on his wooden leg to Charlie, and pulled him aside. "I've taken a cotton to you, Charlie. You have a mind like a steel trap and the instincts to match, so you know what must be done. The Watch needs a scapegoat."

Charlie stiffened. "Balderdash. Sir, if the mayor really wants to put people's minds at ease, he should shut down Demon Gate and kick out the demons."

Farrier corrected the angry teen. "Dimensionals. You may call them whatever you wish when you're not wearing the uniform, but on duty, you shall refer to them as Dimensionals."

Charlie nodded. "But we've taken a dangerous one off the street. If one of my men started the fire, it was an accident."

The commander held up the paper. "Tell that to the press. They're having a field day, calling my Demon Watch *irresponsible*. I need to give them someone. I gave you the opportunity to control your squad's fate, but it seems I must handle this myself. A leader has to take responsibility for his squad's actions."

Ehrich couldn't let his friend lose his job over this. He inched forward.

Charlie stopped him. "It was Louis."

Ehrich's eyes widened but he kept quiet. Farrier leaned forward.

"You sure it was Louis?"

Guilt slapped Ehrich on both cheeks, making them hot and flushed. He could make things right just by speaking up, but his lips felt like they had been nailed shut.

Charlie continued. "Tell the mayor Louis went rogue. Whatever you want to tell him. Louis might not even make it to the end of the day, so he won't argue."

Farrier crossed his arms over his chest, exposing the scars along his forearms. "Tarnation, I'm impressed. You are a genuine politician."

"What happened in the Bowery was a tragedy, but it was Louis's fault, and Louis's alone." Charlie stood at attention.

"Do you concur with your squad leader?" Farrier asked of the others.

They nodded.

Farrier looked directly into Ehrich's eyes. "Well, Mr. Weisz?"

"Doesn't matter what he thinks," Charlie jumped in. "I'm the squad leader and that's exactly what happened."

The commander stroked his beard, considering the angles. Finally, he nodded. "That should do."

"Then is my squad off the hook, sir?" Charlie asked.

"Not quite," Farrier answered. He fixed his gaze on Ehrich and smiled.

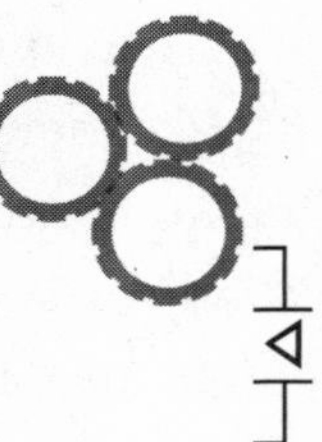

BURIAL DUTY

The shovel blade bit into the hard earth. Ehrich grunted as he loosened the dirt. Wooden crosses pockmarked the emerald lawn in front of the looming six-story brick structure that housed the Demon Gate facilities. Just beyond the ivy-covered building were the staff dormitories, the training facilities, and the short building that was the entrance to Ninth Circle, the underground prison.

"We wouldn't be here if you had just given the commander the answer he wanted," the reedy Wilhelm complained.

"What answer is that?" Charlie asked, leaning on his shovel.

"You know." Wilhelm wiped the sweat from his brow and nodded at Ehrich. "Even a trainee would be a better hunter than Ehrich."

"You all agree?" Charlie asked.

Margaret kept digging. "Doesn't matter what I think."

Gino shrugged. "Wilhelm gripes as soon as the sun rises, and then when sun sets, he complains there's not enough time to do his work."

"Quiet, Gino," Wilhelm growled. "Farrier knew Ehrich was in Bandit's Roost. That's why he gave us burial duty."

"Could be worse," Ehrich pointed out. "At least we're not human guinea pigs for the mad scientist." He nodded to the island north of Devil's Island, where the peak of a round tower was clearly visible.

Wilhelm jammed his shovel into the dirt. "It's because of you that my friend is fighting for his life right now."

"Enough," Charlie barked. "Back to work."

Wilhelm yanked his shovel out of the earth. "Louis deserves better."

Margaret grunted. "Hey! I'd like to get these pine boxes into the ground before the stench makes me puke." She motioned at the two coffins perched on top of each other on a large wooden wagon.

The squad resumed digging.

Ehrich leaned over to Charlie and whispered, "I still say that you could have handed me over to Farrier. Might have made your life easier."

"Wilhelm could have, too, but the squad comes first. Ride this out. If Louis lives, Wilhelm will get off your back."

Ehrich felt the heat of the sun on his nape, but that was nothing compared to the intensity of Wilhelm's glare. He turned his back on the German boy and redoubled his efforts to dig the grave.

A ship's horn tooted in the distance. Ehrich peered in the

direction of the sound. To the east of the island, a fleet of ships was moored at the docks on the Brooklyn side of the East River. Their masts rose high in the air like a forest of barren trees. A vessel laden with goods floated along the briny water, passing a steam-powered barge. Billows of black smoke filled the air as the flat craft rolled against the wake of the larger ship, then chugged toward Devil's Island.

"Death barge," Charlie announced. "Guess we've got more bodies to bury."

Wilhelm groaned. Margaret shook her head. Gino chuckled. "Most people are itching to get off this island, but the dead can't seem to stay away."

"Ehrich, you're with me," said Charlie. "We'll collect the new bodies. You three, finish digging. I want the boxes in the ground by the time I get back."

Charlie and Ehrich hauled the remaining coffins off the wagon and placed them near the gravesites. Then they pushed the large cart toward the pier. By the time they arrived at the dock, the death barge had arrived. A young man with a hint of facial hair greeted them. He motioned to the crewmen who were hoisting a pine box on to the pier.

"Get it on, quick," he ordered.

The crewmen grunted as they hauled the casket toward the wagon. The teen stroked his thin moustache.

"Got a fresh body for you fellas. Better get a move on. Rush order."

Charlie waved him off. "Man alive, what's the rush? He's as cold as a wagon tire, isn't he? He'll still be as cold tomorrow when we bury him."

"Ain't a he. It's a she. And she ain't for the ground."

"What do you mean?" Ehrich asked. "What else are we going to do with a body?"

His friend stiffened. "Oh no. Double check the log."

"Sorry, guys. The paperwork's right."

Ehrich glanced at his friend. "Where do we have to take the body?"

"Demon Gate."

An Unlikely Reunion

Demon Gate stood six floors above ground. The top floor was home to Farrier's administration offices while the floors below were where the bulk of the action took place. The dormitories for Dimensionals awaiting approval to enter New York took up the space of two floors. Divided by female and male, the living quarters here made the Lower East Side tenements look like palaces. In dank open areas, people sat on suitcases and slept on saggy cots. Below the dormitories, on the facility's second and third floors, Demon Watch doctors monitored the new arrivals in the quarantine section. Newcomers spent their first two weeks in New York in these cramped quarters, while doctors tested them for communicable diseases.

Ehrich and Charlie headed to the facility's ground floor, the Dimensionals' entry point—Demon Gate. He and Charlie pushed the wagon through the wide corridor leading to the central processing area.

Charlie sniffed the air. "I don't know how the guys down here get used to the stench."

Ehrich winced at the rank odour of decaying bodies. He spotted a fog of his own breath. "Why is it so cold?" he asked.

"Bodies decay slower when it's chilly," Charlie said, releasing steam from his mouth.

Arc lamps lit the corridor. As the teens rolled the wagon ahead, Ehrich heard faint whispers. A chorus of inaudible voices echoed up and down the hall.

"Who's doing that?" Ehrich asked, looking up. "Doesn't sound like it's coming from quarantine."

Charlie shook his head. "Some say they're coming from the Dimensionals waiting to come through Demon Gate. Others say they're the voices of the dead. No one knows for sure. Sometimes we can catch glimpses of them. You can hear them and some of the guards have seen one or two."

"Like spirits?"

"Yeah. I never got used to it."

"Charlie, you had to work here? When?"

"If you want to lead a squad, you have to get up close and personal with the Dimensionals. Maybe someday you'll have a chance to do this."

Ehrich shook his head. "Not if Farrier has his way."

Charlie laughed. "Yeah, he hasn't taken a shine to you."

"I guess I should have 'concurred' with him."

They both shared a laugh. Ehrich forced himself to laugh a little louder so he could drown out the incessant whispering.

At the end of the corridor stood two guards stationed outside Demon Gate's entry. Each one wore an elephant gas mask with an accordion hose attached to an air pack on their hip. The breathing masks filtered the stench of the dead. The guards tipped their teslatron rifles up at the approaching pair, greeting their arrival. They pushed open the double doors leading into Demon Gate's chamber.

Ehrich stiffened when he entered. Throughout the cavernous room, he spotted ghostly figures wafting between the electrical towers. In the centre of the room loomed a giant Faraday Cage constructed of non-conductive mesh walls. This cage was designed to nullify any weapon technology that Dimensionals might bring with them. A bored clerk sat at a massive oak desk in front of the cage. He had cotton wads stuffed up his nose.

Around the room, Demon Gate guards stood along the walls. They all wore elephant gas masks. Ehrich wished he had one right now. On the other side of the Faraday Cage, two operators stood behind control panels. Thick cables snaked across the stone ground and connected with the twelve tepee-shaped towers. These were Demon Gate's generators, but on closer inspection, Ehrich realized they were not electrical transformers; they were powered by something else. A corpse stood in a sarcophagus within the heart of each tower. Eleven of the towers glowed with necro energy, the energy that corpses produced, but the twelfth flickered, dimmer than the rest. Inside the tower, a skeleton threatened to disintegrate into dust.

Within the Faraday Cage, an emaciated green-skinned immigrant stood with an overstuffed leather valise in one hand. His grey hair was barely visible under a black toque. He wore an ankle-length brown robe with a yellowed paper pinned to his breast. The paper was his entry visa. The clerk skimmed the note.

"What's the name of your sponsor again?"

"Name? He Mr. Siren-tee."

"The note says 'Serenity'. How do you say his name?"

"Siren-tee. Mr. Siren-tee."

"Send him to quarantine," the nasally voiced clerk ordered.

One of the operators punched a button on the console. The gate on the cage swung open. Unsure, the newcomer slowly stepped out. The bewildered man tapped the page on his chest. "My paper. I have. I Piotravisk. My name Piotravisk."

"They will deal with that in processing. Out that way." The agent over-enunciated every word in a condescending tone.

"My friend. She here. She with Piotravisk." The man in the brown robe glanced at the Faraday Cage.

"Yeah, yeah. If we can get to her, she'll join you soon. If not, you'll see her in general quarters in two weeks."

"My friend. She come soon?"

The clerk simply waved to one of the guards who escorted Piotravisk through a door that lead to the stairs up to the quarantine level.

The clerk smoothed his thinning hair as he stepped around the desk to greet Ehrich and Charlie. He pulled out his cotton nose plugs and shook Charlie's hand with the hand holding the plugs.

"About time. We put in the request a week ago."

Charlie wiped his hand on his trousers. "We just move the bodies. We don't round them up."

"Smells pretty fresh," the clerk said. "Load it up there."

"I'm pulling rank, Ehrich," Charlie said.

"It's a two-man job," Ehrich protested.

"And you're just the two men to do it." He flashed a flirtatious smile at one of the masked guards with long, frizzy, brown hair.

"Pray tell, what are you going to do?"

"I'm a bit busy talking with... with..." Charlie nodded at the guard with the elephant mask.

"Frank," he answered, his voice muffled.

"Oh. Sorry. I thought you were... Never mind. Just get to work, Ehrich."

"Okay, okay." Ehrich rolled the corpse wagon toward the tower in question. As he moved past the other towers, he noticed each corpse was in a different state of decomposition. They all wore unisex gowns. Most of the bodies were still intact while some appeared as if their rotting flesh were falling off the bone.

He opened the standing coffin's glass lid. If possible, the sickly sweet stench from the skeleton grew even worse. Ehrich grabbed the arm, and the fragile bone broke off in his hands. He covered his mouth to keep from vomiting. He cursed his friend as he unloaded the rest of the bones and used the smock to gather the detritus at the bottom of the sarcophagus.

He opened the pine box and his brow furrowed at the sight of the female corpse inside. She reeked of heavy perfume and decay. The gash across her throat and her empty eye sockets were unmistakeable—Ole Lukoje's reanimated corpse. An unlikely reunion, Ehrich wondered if there was a mother or father, even a sister or brother, to mourn this woman. Did her family know the horrible way she died? Did they know her body was to be used as a fuel cell? Or did the coroner conveniently neglect to inform them? He knew the answer and he didn't like it. He gently slipped his hands under her armpits and pulled her out.

"What's taking so long?" Charlie asked.

Moving the corpse was no easy task; her stiff body had a slippery sheen.

Charlie turned to the others and said, “If you want to dance with the dead, she has to face you.”

Laughter echoed through the room. Ehrich gritted his teeth, ignoring the jeers, and placed the body in the sarcophagus, then rolled the wagon away from the tower. The dead powered the tall towers, but no ordinary corpse would do. Like the eyeless woman, the corpses had to have died in a violent manner to be effective batteries for Demon Gate. Ehrich was disgusted at the idea that these victims had their lives ripped away, only to be further abused in death. He closed the glass lid and stepped back. He tore a bit of his shirttail as he tried to recall the blessing he heard at the funerals his rabbi father used to oversee—“*Baruch dayan ha'emet.*”

An operator stepped behind the console and flipped the switch. The tower glowed a faint blue, gaining in intensity until it was the brightest tower in the cavern.

In an instant, ghostly voices filled the room. A phantom rushed at Ehrich, her mouth open in a scream. He flinched as her wispy form went right through his body and sent shivers up his spine. He turned and she was gone from sight. The clerk signalled the operator to flip another switch and she complied. Sparks flew across the Faraday Cage as bolts of blue energy danced from tower to cage. For a flash, Ehrich could glimpse a world beyond, within the mesh walls. Then an ebony-skinned girl appeared in the cage.

A suede corset hugged her muscular body. The drawstrings in front exposed a linen shirt underneath. Thigh-high boots with rust-brown stains accentuated her slender legs. She tugged the black choker around her neck, revealing a pearl cameo with the faint impression of an eye.

The girl carried in her hand a leather-bound book. One of the Demon Gate guards rolled a tall, flat device in front of the cage. He flipped a switch on the side of the machine, and the thin black screen lit up. An X-ray sort of image revealed what was under the clothes of the new arrival. Her skeleton frame appeared human, but the book in her hand appeared to be a device. Ehrich could see a collection of gears, cogs, and circuits beneath the bindings.

"Pass me the book," the clerk ordered.

She obeyed, sliding the thick volume through a slot in the mesh gate.

"I'll need that back." She spoke with a hint of an accent, as if she had grown up around English speakers who had learned the language second hand.

"Not until we've examined it," the clerk said. "Where are your papers?"

She drew her papers from inside her left boot and handed them to the clerk. He ignored her as he tried to open the book, but the lock held the cover shut. He gave up on the second try and snatched the papers from the girl to compare it to the paperwork on his desk.

"State your name," he said.

"Amina."

"Name of your sponsor?"

"Mr. Serenity."

The processing clerk raised his gaze, eyes widening. "You sure about that? Your friend pronounced it differently."

She shrugged. "Probably his accent. Serenity is right."

He checked his logbook, and flipped to the questionnaire. "What is Mr. Serenity's profession?"

"He owns a business."

"What's the name?"

"Mr. Serenity's Museum of Curiosities. Is this important?"

"Tell me which direction the bedroom window in your childhood home faced."

"East."

"What was the maiden name of your mother's third cousin?"

"Mwindaji."

"Tell me the number of steps on the front porch of your current residence."

She tugged at the leather choker around her neck. "Three."

The clerk eyed the questionnaire, then took a long look at Amina before he spoke. "Clear." The cage gate opened. "Take her to quarantine, Frank. Unless your friend still wants to chat with you." He winked at Charlie.

"I'm good," Charlie said.

"When do I get my book back?" Amina asked.

"Not my department," the clerk grunted as he turned his back on her. He tossed the book at Ehrich. "This one's for the mad scientist."

Ehrich turned the book over. A stamp on the spine made him catch his breath and his hand moved instinctively to his shirt.

"That's not our job," Charlie argued.

The clerk shot back, "If you have time to carry a corpse here, you have time to run this across."

"Not a problem, Charlie," Ehrich interrupted quickly. "I'll take it over."

His friend turned. "We're not errand boys."

"Beats digging graves," Ehrich said.

Charlie narrowed his gaze. "Damn you for thinking of it first."

The clerk stuffed the cotton wads up his nostrils. "If you two are through gossiping, clear this mess out of here."

Charlie tilted the wagon so that the remains of the corpse spilled on the ground. "Oops. Guess you'll have to do a little cleaning yourself." He led the way out of Demon Gate.

In the hall, Ehrich drew out the medallion under his shirt. When he touched the metal amulet, he felt the eerie presence of his brother.

The trinket always triggered Ehrich's memory of the last moments of his brother's life. Sometimes, he saw the knife go into Dash. Other times, he felt Dash near him. Today, he could hear his brother's voice gnawing at his conscience. He closed his eyes and held his breath, counting to ten until the voice faded away.

He opened his eyes and examined the insignia on the medallion. Right down to the curve of the snake's tail on the lion, the chimera on the cover matched the one on the book's spine.

THE MAD SCIENTIST

"Come, come," Madame Mancini wheezed.

The milky-eyed woman ushered Ehrich and two other people into her parlour. He glanced around the tiny room, noting the large cabinet set against the bare wall. In the centre was a round table with a red tablecloth covering it. A lit candle provided the only illumination in the dark place. The medium beckoned the trio to sit. They obeyed as the woman tucked a stray black hair under her kerchief and joined them at the table.

"I see much pain in all of you. No need to worry. Tonight, we will bring you some peace and comfort. Did you bring the items?"

Everyone produced a different item. Ehrich reached into his shirt and pulled the medallion hanging around his neck. When he touched the copper amulet, he heard the voice of his brother Dash in his mind. "Ehrich... Ehrich..." He hesitated.

"This was all I had," he said.

Madame Mancini clucked, "Perfect. I can see you are troubled, but tonight you will find the answers you seek. Place the item on the table."

He obeyed and Dash's voice faded away. The pale woman beside him pulled out a comb. The man with the handlebar moustache drew out a handkerchief.

"She only used this once before she shrugged her mortal coil," he said as if he were apologizing for some failing.

"Perfect," the plump woman told the moustached man. "Place the item on the table. We will see which spirit is drawn to them."

The medium placed a hand bell in the middle of the items.

"Spiritualism is an inexact science. I must warn you the spirits decide if they wish to speak, not I. If they do decide to join us, we will know through this bell. We cannot force them and I cannot guarantee you will all have a chance to connect with your departed loved ones. If you are prepared for this, then we can proceed."

The trio nodded.

"Tell me your names," she ordered.

Ehrich turned to the pale woman beside him. She murmured, "My name is Katherine."

The man with the moustache answered, "John."

Ehrich gave his name.

"Now that we have met each other, let us join hands," Madame Mancini said as she blew out the candle.

Ehrich couldn't see anything, but he felt the stiff hand of the rotund medium as she chanted. "Spirits of the other world, we call you to this room. Come to us. We desire to speak with you."

Silence.

"We beseech you to come here. Your loved ones want to— Wait. Do you feel that?"

Something brushed against the back of Ehrich's neck. He sat up. "I did."

"Spirit, are you in the room with us? Ring the bell if you are."

Ding.

"Who do you wish to speak with? Your wife? Your husband? Your brother?"

Ding.

Madame Mancini asked, "Who among you has the brother?"

Ehrich answered, "I do. His name is Dash."

"Dash, are you here? Ring twice for yes."

Ding, ding.

"Your brother's presence is strong. Oh, spirit of Dash, your brother is here."

"Are you sure?" Ehrich asked.

"Speak through me, spirit. Come into my body so I may be your voice," the old woman moaned.

The sounds of the bell and the crashing of metal against wood. It was as if the spirit was working its way around the room.

Then the old woman's voice changed to a child's voice, meek and timid. "Ehrich, is that you, my brother?"

"Dash?"

"Yes, yes. Why have you brought me here?"

"I wanted to know if you were okay. Are you?"

"Perfect. I've never been happier in all my life."

Ehrich gripped the seer's hand tighter. She didn't squeeze back. "I have a question."

"What do you want to know?"

"The medallion you wore. Where did you get it from?"

Silence.

"I've never seen the medallion before. Dash, I want to know

what it means to you."

"I took it from our grandmother's room when she wasn't looking."

"Grandmother? Which grandmother?"

Silence.

"Are you sure, Dash?"

The bell rang three times, then silence. Ehrich gripped the hard hand of the seer.

"I'm sorry, Ehrich, but the spirit has gone," Madame Mancini's voice sounded like her old self. "He was upset about the medallion. I felt strong pangs of guilt. Maybe because he stole it and he didn't want you to know from where."

"Get him back. I want answers," Ehrich demanded as he gripped the woman's hand.

"The spirits come when they choose."

"Bring him back," he ordered. He yanked on the woman's hand, but her arm stretched as he pulled. The hand stayed in his, but her grip felt unnatural.

"What are you doing?" the medium shouted. "Let go."

A hand grabbed his arm, as if it were searching for something. He flinched, holding on to the seer's hand. Commotion in the room. A pair of hands grabbed his arm.

"Help!" he yelled, leaping to his feet. "A spirit has me!"

Pandemonium set in as the room filled with the crashes and screams of people trying to flee the space. A door opened and light flooded into the darkened room, revealing Madame Mancini in a tug of war with Ehrich over a fake arm that was strapped to her side. The prosthetic matched another one strapped to her other side. She looked like a Hindu goddess.

"Charlatan!" Ehrich shouted.

"Get out!" Madame Mancini screamed.

"You rang the bell yourself! You're a fake!"

"Out!" She waved her real arms at him.

He grabbed Dash's medallion and left.

Ehrich stared at the medallion in his hand as he waited for the bridge between Devil's Island and Randall's Island to span the strait. The mighty metal structure uncoiled from its snail-shell shape and stretched across the water to meet the other bridge which was also uncurling. Dash's voice in his mind was like that second bridge, reaching from beyond, but Ehrich dreaded the meeting of the two. He shut his eyes and counted to ten until the voice of his brother faded away.

The bridge halves met over the rushing water and Ehrich stepped on the deck to cross over to Randall's Island, which was home to the mad scientist's labs. The guards stood at attention, watching his approach, unaccustomed to visitors. Rumour had it the mad scientist preferred his privacy.

He walked along the algae-covered stone path toward the looming white tower at the centre of the island. Around the six-story tower were smaller areas for lodging and labs for assistants to work in, but whatever they did in these tiny labs was nothing compared to the products invented in the tower. The mad scientist was responsible for coming up with the hunters' weapons against the Dimensionals, along with the technology that controlled Demon Gate. Some whispered he had inventions which would change the world.

None of that mattered to Ehrich. He only needed to learn what was in the Dimensional's book. If the tome could shed any light on the connection between Dash and the medallion, then maybe he could find some peace of mind.

He reached the base of the building, where a guard stood. She surveyed him up and down, taking in his hunter's duster.

"What's your business here?" she asked.

"We took something off a Dimensional. It might be a weapon."

"It looks like a book."

Ehrich grinned. "Yeah, that's what I said, and now I'm here instead of there."

She shook her head. "Bureaucrats. Okay, go on up. I think he's on the fourth floor today."

"Thanks!" Ehrich said. He pushed the door open and headed into the lobby. The floor was white marble, and a spiral staircase ran up and around the circular wall. Chandeliers hung from above, providing illumination, but the skylight provided plenty of sunlight to brighten the area. Ehrich began to climb the stairs, taking a quick peek at each level as he went up. The main level seemed to be living quarters. The second floor housed what appeared to be servants' quarters. The third level housed laboratories where inventions were in various states of completion. When he arrived on the fourth level, he found more devices, but these seemed to be less finished than the ones below.

Giant towers hooked to thick cables populated the room. A six-foot tall man, thin as a rail, boasting an impressive waxed moustache, and wearing an impeccable three-piece suit paced between the towers. In the middle of the transformers, the inventor adjusted the connections with the kind of precision of a man who knew exactly what he wanted. This was the mad scientist—Nikola Tesla.

"What do you want?" Tesla asked, without even turning around. His English was like a country road, broken up with an eastern European accent similar to Ehrich's parents'. Though they were Hungarian, their language patterns were similar to Tesla's Serbian accent.

"Commander Farrier would like you to examine this device. He thinks we can learn something about a new Dimensional."

"Put the book on the table. When I have the time, I will take a look."

"He told me to tell you this is a high-priority item," Ehrich said, hoping Tesla wouldn't test his lie.

The mad scientist walked from one transformer to another, waving his hand dismissively. He continued inspecting the tall towers in the room, completely ignoring Ehrich for several minutes. Copper wires wound around a thick cylinder, and a doughnut-shaped mechanism sat atop the entire pole. The base of the tower seemed to house a motor of some sort.

"Sir," Ehrich insisted. "We really need to know what this book does."

"What are you still doing here?" Tesla asked. "You can remind your commander his domain does not extend to my facilities."

"I was told not to leave until you had examined this device," he lied.

"You will be standing there a long time then."

"Sir, this won't take more than a few minutes. He just wants to know what is inside the book."

Tesla ignored him. Ehrich decided to up the stakes. He walked over to one of the transformers and began to examine the connections. This got Tesla's attention immediately.

"Get away from there, young man." His Serbian accent

seemed to become more prominent under stress.

"I thought I could be of some use to you. Help you finish this so you can test the device. What if I touch this cable?"

"No. Don't. Promise you will not touch anything in the room."

"Gladly. As soon as you look at this book."

"Ah, extortion—the game of amateurs."

"If it works..." Ehrich said.

"What is your name?"

"Ehrich Weisz."

"Now that I think of it, you can help me with a task. Stand in the middle of the room. Yes, on the platform." The thin man took the book and walked over to the table, where he set it down.

Ehrich began to regret his decision to bluff the mad scientist. He recalled the many stories hunters had told about the man's need for guinea pigs. He looked at the Tesla coils in the room with their mushroom heads. They hummed with energy.

"Sir, if you look at the book, I can be on my way."

"Yes, Ehrich, I will certainly look at it, right after I test the equipment."

"What kind of test are you running?" Ehrich asked, trying to hide his mounting fear.

"This won't take long, Ehrich. I can't decide which is more dramatic, 25,000 volts or 50,000."

"What are you going to do with that much electricity?"

"Why, boy, I'm going to run it through your body."

Ehrich gulped, but didn't budge. "And you say it won't take long?"

"Hardly, but the electricity may sting."

"Then you'd better get going because Commander Farrier is

desperate to find out what is in the book."

Tesla furrowed his eyebrows and turned away.

"You are sure you want to go through with this, young man? This is your final chance to step off. I've never tried the Tesla coils at 50,000 volts, so we are both in uncharted waters."

"What is the point of this experiment, Mr. Tesla?"

"Very simple, Mr. Weisz. I want to determine what voltage level is considered dangerous for AC power."

Ehrich glanced nervously at the towers one more time. If Tesla had meant to scare him off, the ploy was working. He inched toward the edge of the platform, but he caught a glimpse of the man smiling. He moved back to the centre of the platform.

"Then you might want to try 50,000 volts so you can erase all doubts," Ehrich said.

"You are certain?"

Ehrich wanted to scream "no," but he needed to find out what was in the book. He nodded.

"Very well," Tesla said. He turned to the console and dialled up several knobs. The surrounding towers began to hum in a high-pitched whine, almost sounding like a swarm of bees buzzing in unison. Ehrich stiffened and stared at Tesla, daring the man to go through with his bluff.

"I'm ready," Ehrich said.

Tesla cracked a smile and turned the dial. Lightning leapt from one of the Tesla coils and danced up and down Ehrich's arm. He jumped back but stayed on the platform as electricity from another tower found his other arm. He watched the blue light dance up and down his flesh, but he didn't feel any heat, just a tickle as his arm hair stood on end. The rest of the towers unleashed their impotent fury on Ehrich, and he stretched out his arms to catch the lightning, laughing as he watched the dancing storm. Then, one after the other, the towers powered down and the light show was done. All that remained was a beaming Ehrich.

Tesla tapped his chin three times. "You are quite determined to learn what is in this book."

"I'm following the commander's orders."

"Ah yes, the commander and his vigilance against the evils that would invade our dimension. Let's satisfy his curiosity."

Ehrich stepped off the platform and joined Tesla at the table. The thin man examined the spine of the book, running his hands along the insignia, then over the lock mechanism.

"We tried to open the lock, but there was no keyhole," Ehrich explained.

"Yes, I can see. The problem is the mechanism was designed to appear like a lock so you would not guess its true purpose." He grasped the top and bottom edges of the lock and twisted. The brass casing didn't budge. He turned it the other way. Finally, he lifted and twisted. The entire mechanism shifted one quarter to the right. The book responded with a low hum. Tesla turned the mechanism back to its original spot and the noise faded.

"I can tell you right now, it is not a book."

"What is it?" Ehrich asked.

"I cannot even fathom a guess. This may take some time. Come back Friday morning at nine. Sharp. I will have need of your services, and I will have the answers you seek."

With that, he took the book across the room, counting his steps in groups of three, and disappeared down the hall. Bemused by the scientist's eccentricities, Ehrich couldn't help but smile.

PARLOUR TRICKS

Margaret rifled through Ehrich's footlocker in the dorm while Gino kept watch at the doorway. On Ehrich's bed, Wilhelm was flipping through a book—the autobiography of a French magician named Robert Houdin. Ehrich's other books on stage magic were strewn across his bed.

"Get a look at this," Margaret said as she held up a pair of handcuffs. "No keys to go with the cuffs."

"Guess he thinks he's a real magician," Gino quipped. "I mean, look at the way he *disappeared* from work."

Margaret laughed. "Yeah."

Wilhelm raised his hand for silence. "Get this. His hero is Robert Houdin. The guy apparently works with automatons. Listen to this: 'All thoughtful persons will understand the difficulty of making my automaton perform so many different movements, as when it stands on its legs and moves its head to the right and left. They will also see that this animal drinks, dabbles with its bill, quacks like the living duck.' A mechanical duck. Talk about hogwash."

Gino joked, "Well, you know what they say. If it looks like a duck and sounds like a duck, it's probably an automaton."

Margaret held up the handcuff keys. "Found them."

"Toss them both here," Wilhelm said. She did.

He tested the shackles, snapping them open and closed.

Gino hissed, "He's here."

⊃══□⊏

Ehrich strolled into the dorm but picked up the pace when he spotted his possessions splayed across the bed and floor. "What do you think you're doing? Those are my personal things."

Wilhelm smiled. "We thought since you left us with a mess to clean up, we would return the favour."

Gino and Margaret laughed.

"Not funny," Ehrich said.

"That is what I said when Charlie came back from Demon Gate and said you had taken off and left us to finish your work." Wilhelm kicked a book off the bed.

"Charlie didn't seem to mind."

"He didn't do the digging," Margaret quipped.

Gino jumped in. "You know what, *Air-ee*," he said, deliberately mispronouncing Ehrich's name as he always did when he wanted to get under someone's skin. "You hurt our feelings. When we're on patrol, you're the first to freelance and leave us to save your hide. I'm starting to think you don't like us."

Wilhelm swung his legs off the bed. "Easy, Gino. That's too far. I'm sure Ehrich knows the squad comes first."

"Just reminding him of that," Gino muttered.

Ehrich picked up the books on the floor and started to put them back into his footlocker. Margaret didn't bother moving out of his way.

Wilhelm handed Ehrich the Robert Houdin autobiography. "Hey, we're just fooling around, Ehrich. I know you enjoy magic, but just don't try to get all Houdin-y on us. No more parlour tricks."

Gino guffawed. "Houdini! I like that. A good Italian name."

Margaret nodded. "Why don't you show us one of your feats of magic?"

"Maybe you can pull a rabbit out of a box," Gino said. "I always wanted to know how they did it."

"A magician doesn't give away his secrets," Ehrich said.

"Come on, Houdini," Wilhelm said. "Amaze us."

"Another time."

Margaret cocked her head to one side, letting her long dark hair fall over her eye. "It's the least you could do for us."

"Forget the magic, Houdini," Wilhelm said. "How about an escape trick? Let's see you get out of the shackles." He picked up the handcuffs from the bed.

"Yeah," Gino chimed in. "Let's watch an escape artist at work."

Margaret agreed. "And when you escape, we'll clean this up."

"Fine, fine. Let's do this." Ehrich held out his hands for Wilhelm to cuff him. The German boy shook his head and motioned Ehrich to turn around. Ehrich did and Wilhelm cuffed him behind his back. He took his time, making the cuffs as tight as possible.

"What are you doing?" Ehrich asked.

"Hold on...just about..." he grunted, manipulating the shackles. The shackles clicked together; then the rasp of another sound, which Ehrich couldn't quite make out. Wilhelm was up to something, but Ehrich didn't know what. He was pretty sure he knew why.

"Tight enough for you, Houdini?"

"They're fine," Ehrich said, gritting his teeth to shut out the pain of the metal shackles cutting into his wrist.

Wilhelm stepped around and held up the handcuff key, but something was wrong. The end had been snapped off.

"What did you do, Wilhelm?" Ehrich demanded as he lurched forward.

"You might have a harder time getting out of the shackles than you did getting out of work."

Gino and Margaret laughed as they all backed away from Ehrich, who struggled with the cuffs. He let the tension in his shoulders go slack as he curled into a ball on the floor and stepped through his shackled arms so that he could assess what had been done to the cuffs. Wilhelm had snapped the key off in the lock mechanism.

"Bravo!" Wilhelm mocked as he clapped.

"He's not out yet," Margaret said.

Ehrich ignored them as he slid under the covers of his cot. He had no intention of showing his secrets to Wilhelm. Under the blanket, Ehrich reached into his shoe and pulled out the lock-pick set he kept in his right heel. If he could loosen the key end from the mechanism, he might have a shot at getting free.

Gino laughed, "Oh look, he's suddenly shy."

"Guess he thought it was too easy," Margaret said.

"Then let's make it harder," Wilhelm said. He lunged at Ehrich and grabbed the blanket. Gino jumped to the other side of the bed. The boys twisted the blanket and wrapped the makeshift flannel rope around Ehrich's arms and body. They tied Ehrich to the bed frame while Margaret rolled up another blanket from the nearby cot. She tied the blanket around the foot of the bed and his legs so Ehrich couldn't bring his feet to his hands. Once he was completely trussed up, the trio admired their handiwork. Ehrich squirmed against his bonds, but he couldn't set himself free.

"This is boring," Wilhelm said. "What do you say, Gino?"

"I *concur*."

"Margaret?"

"I'm not impressed so far," she said.

Wilhelm nodded. "Then we should get out of here." They walked away.

"You can't leave me here!" Ehrich called after them as he squirmed against the bonds, trying to loosen the blankets. A moment later, just as he had started to make progress, Charlie entered the dorm and saw his friend's predicament. The squad leader rushed to the bed and untied the knotted blanket around Ehrich's feet.

"What happened?"

"I was trying to show off an escape trick. Hit a snag." Ehrich wasn't about to get into any more trouble with Wilhelm.

Charlie untied Ehrich's arms. "Good thing you have a job on Demon Watch because you'd starve if you tried to work as a dime-store magician."

"Thanks for the vote of confidence."

"They left you here?"

Ehrich didn't want to tell Charlie the real story, but he sensed his friend was fishing for more details. "Wilhelm saw my book and wanted me to show what I had learned."

"They were pretty upset when you didn't come back to finish digging the graves."

"Wilhelm's never liked me, so it's hard to tell."

"Good point. He was pretty close to Louis."

"How is Louis?"

Charlie shook his head. "The doctor says he might not make it to the end of the week."

"I'm sorry."

"Big price to pay to bring in a demon," Charlie said. "But we did our job as a team."

Ehrich picked up the broken key and used the end to clear the jammed lock. He was careful not to damage the mechanism as he pushed.

"You know it was Wilhelm who spotted you in the Bowery. He was the one who alerted me. If not for him, you might be where Louis is."

"I didn't know."

"He's not one to brag—he's more of a complainer. But at the end of the day, he knows no matter what he thinks of his teammates, the squad comes first. Whatever happens in here is your business, but out there, we're a team. Our lives depend on this. You know what I'm talking about, Houdini?"

Ehrich's eyes widened. Charlie had heard the exchange in the dorm and allowed the squad to continue. He was sending Ehrich a message.

"I can't undo what happened to Louis," Ehrich said. "I'm sorry I went freelance. I should have stuck with the squad."

"You have a habit of forgetting we are a squad. Doesn't hurt to let the others know you still remember. Listen, we have to dig more graves tomorrow. I was thinking of giving us all some downtime in the morning. Let the others sleep in. It'd be nice if someone got a head start on the graves, you know?"

Ehrich nodded. Charlie patted him on the leg and walked out. Alone, Ehrich was able to spring the lock on his shackles. Always when he was alone, he could do it—never under pressure. He picked up his things from the ground, feeling about as alone as he did when he first arrived in this dimension. While he might look like the others, he knew deep down he was not the same. The weight of this made him long for home.

SABOTAGE

The week had passed by slowly for Ehrich. For a couple of days, he reached a détente with Wilhelm by doing more than his share of the administrative punishments. They had moved from burial duty to loading food shipments for Demon Watch. The squad began to joke with each other. Ehrich even learned to embrace the nickname the others had bestowed on him.

"Houdini, want to wave your wand and levitate these crates so I don't break my back lifting them?" Gino said.

"Houdini, make this week disappear so we can get back to our real jobs," Charlie joked.

"Ladies and gentlemen, I give you Houdini, the world's worst escape artist," Margaret said, "Can't get out of handcuffs—can't get out of burial duty".

Ehrich took a bow and said, "Thank you, thank you. I'll be here all week for your entertainment. If my sleeves start spitting feathers, don't worry. Nothing up there, I swear."

The others laughed. Even Wilhelm cracked a small smile.

Their mood all changed Thursday, when Louis died. That night, a dark cloud settled over the squad as they had lost one of their own. No one felt like joking or talking. Wilhelm's temper turned black as he perched on the edge of his bed. He shrugged off Charlie's attempt to console him. The raggedy man would have to answer for the slaying of a hunter now, and Wilhelm wanted to execute the punishment personally. Since he could not get his hands on the prisoner in Ninth Circle, he lashed out at the people around him.

"Houdini, do us all a favour and disappear," Wilhelm said. "I don't want to see your ugly face right now."

"Easy, Wilhelm," Margaret said. "We all know the risks of the job." Of all the squad members, she was the most pragmatic. Sometimes, this came across as heartless.

"Shut up, Margaret. Louis was my friend and because of Houdini, he's gone."

Ehrich felt a hole in his stomach growing wider and sucking him into the abyss of guilt. He shouldered the blame for Louis' death, just as he carried the burden of losing Dash.

Gino cut in. "Wilhelm, I was supposed to cover Louis. I'm as much to blame."

Margaret shook her head. "We can't blame anyone but Ole Lukoje. He's the one who attacked Louis. He would have killed Ehrich too."

Wilhelm's face reddened. "Why didn't you just let the freak go through the gateway? If you did, my best friend would be alive right now."

Charlie raised his hands. "Enough! We lost Louis. I'm not

about to lose my entire squad over this. Wilhelm, you need to find a way to get past this."

"Or else what? Will you kick me off? You always side with him." The German boy's anger was too much to contain. He needed a release.

Ehrich put his hand on Charlie's shoulder and pulled him back. "Wilhelm, you can blame me, but this won't bring Louis back. Still, I can see you're hurting and I'm the one who keeps opening the wound, so the best thing is for me to go away. Charlie, I'm taking a leave from the team. Tesla has work for me. I'm not saying I'm making a permanent move, but if Wilhelm and I are apart, maybe the squad can have some peace."

Charlie started to protest, but Ehrich shook his head. Wilhelm needed to deal with his grief, and he couldn't do that as long as Ehrich was around.

"The squad comes first," Ehrich said. He reached out to shake Wilhelm's hand. The German batted his hand away.

The next morning, Ehrich arrived at Tesla's lab at nine sharp. Tesla was dressed in a neatly pressed three-piece suit. He conducted a tour for a group of well-groomed gentlemen who were smoking cigars and admiring the equipment. Ehrich stayed at the back of the room and observed as the Serb explained the workings of his invention.

"You see, gentlemen, what we have here is the next step which will steer us to the future. The AC transformer can generate enough power to light our city's homes and businesses, but at a fraction of the cost of direct current."

The men nodded, but not overly enthusiastically.

"Ah, the question is the one Mr. Edison has planted in your minds. Is AC power safe? I could tell you, but I believe that your eyes may be more receptive than your ears. Mr. Weisz, if you would be so kind as to assist me." Tesla beckoned Ehrich from the back of the room and motioned him to stand on the platform.

The men eyed him warily as he made his way on to the platform in between the towers. They inched back from him and gathered near Tesla by the console.

"What I am about to do is unleash 50,000 volts into this young man and you will see AC is the safest form of electricity on the market today." He dialled up the console, charging up the Tesla coils. Their bee-songs hummed loudly as electricity leapt across the room and danced on Ehrich's skin, lighting him up. The men gasped in horror, then murmured in amazement as Ehrich turned around and showed he was perfectly all right. The men applauded Tesla, thrilled at the demonstration.

The scientist dialled down the coils and invited Ehrich to get off the platform so that the men could examine him. Other than some dirt under his fingernails, Ehrich was none the worse for wear.

"Impressive, Mr. Tesla. It appears to be as safe as you claim," a gentleman in an elegant suit pronounced.

A bearded man in a long waistcoat eyed the contraptions around the room. "I don't know. I think Edison's company has been in operation longer, and they would know what is safe and what is dangerous."

"If you don't believe your eyes, Mr. Gould, perhaps you'd like to try it yourself."

The other potential investors backed off, but the bearded

sceptic rose to the challenge. "Yes, but perhaps we ought to go with a smaller setting in case things go wrong."

"I assure you, sir, the coils are perfectly safe."

Mr. Gould climbed onto the platform. The bearded fellow slipped his hand in and out of his jacket pocket. Ehrich knew enough from his books on magic that amateur prestidigitators often checked their props at the worst moments. This man was up to something, but before Ehrich could warn Tesla, the coils fired up again.

Lightning branches flew from the coils and danced across Mr. Gould's body. Then, suddenly, his jacket erupted into flame and he yelped. The other men shouted. Tesla dialled down the coils while Ehrich slipped off his duster and rushed to Mr. Gould, shoving him down on the platform and smothering the flames. While he did so, he reached into the bearded man's pocket and retrieved a metal box. He palmed it as he helped the investor to his feet.

The others gathered around the room. Mr. Gould dusted himself off. He spoke calmly as he brushed off the soot from his jacket. "As much as I hate to say this, Mr. Edison was correct about AC technology. I believe I shall invest my money elsewhere. I don't know about you gentlemen, but I could do with a shot of whiskey."

The others murmured agreement. Tesla glared at his equipment.

"There is no way this should have happened. Nothing could have sparked a fire. I've tested the coils a thousand times."

Ehrich held out the box. "I think this might have something to do with it."

"Give that back," Mr. Gould ordered.

Tesla snatched the box from Ehrich. "Hmm. An ignition device. Filled with a bit of kerosene and a flint." He turned to the bearded man. "What is the meaning of this, sir?"

"None of your business."

"I think he meant to sabotage your demonstration," Ehrich exclaimed.

Tesla shook his head. "Another one of Edison's spies. Gentlemen, I trust this cheap parlour trick will not stop you from investing in the future."

"Don't listen to him," Mr. Gould sputtered. "AC technology is obviously unsafe."

"You have a horse in this race, Mr. Gould. I don't think your opinion carries the same weight as it did before."

The bearded man fell silent.

"Now that the tomfoolery is over and done with, may I suggest someone else step on the platform so I can demonstrate just how safe my technology is?"

No one else took Tesla up on his offer. The doubt on their faces spoke volumes. While they shunned Mr. Gould, they couldn't afford to take a chance. One by one, they begged off and left the lab. Only the saboteur was left.

Mr. Gould cracked a grin. "Mr. Edison sends his greetings."

Tesla nodded. "Let me return the favour." He reached behind the console and pulled out a volt pistol. He fired it at Mr. Gould's leg and sent shocks up and down the man's body. He twitched as he fell to the ground, howling in pain. Tesla leaned over him. "Tell your employer that if I wanted my technology to hurt others, it wouldn't be that hard."

The man whimpered.

"Mr. Weisz, would you be so kind as to take out the trash?"

"Yes sir." Ehrich grabbed Mr. Gould by the arm, hauled him to his feet, and led him out of the lab.

When Ehrich returned, Tesla sat down on the platform.

"Who is Edison?"

Tesla answered, "Thomas Edison—do you not know that name?"

Ehrich nodded. "He is the one who invented the light bulb, and he's the one trying to get electrical power into New York, isn't he?"

"Direct current energy. An inferior technology which costs twice as much. He's no inventor. He's a businessman who prefers to bully his competition out. I used to work for him when I lived in Budapest. He had some trouble with his German engineers and his European generators. I offered him some improvements to his equipment, and I suggested a better way to deliver energy, but the arrogant man only listened to the sound of his own voice. Now he wants to get an iron grip on all the electrical delivery systems in North America. He sees my AC technology as a threat. He tried to buy out my patents, but I had a champion who refused to give Edison control. Now he wants to discredit me by claiming my technology is dangerous."

"You think the man who set himself on fire works for Edison?"

Tesla nodded as he rubbed his hands together. "This investors' meeting was my chance to get AC technology into the hands of the people. Could you not see the expressions on their faces? They were intrigued until the fire."

"I don't understand, Mr. Tesla. You say the AC technology is cheaper. Shouldn't that be enough for these businessmen?"

"Ah, there is where you are wrong. People have the most difficulty picturing what is yet to be. If you spark their imaginations, you have to create the illusion of what you see but they do not. Make them see the possibilities. My demonstration was to spark their passion, which would in turn lead to their investments. In other words, I had to put on a show. Sadly, it was not a very good one."

"You'll have other chances," Ehrich said.

"Do you know how hard I had to work to convince these men to come today? No one has taken me seriously since George Westinghouse."

"Who?"

"My original business partner."

"What happened to him?"

"I firmly believe that Edison had him killed. Mr. Westinghouse was travelling through the Bowery when a fight broke out. A ruffian spooked the coach's horses and they panicked. The coach overturned, crushing Mr. Westinghouse. He died from his injuries. I tried to tell people the accident was actually Edison's ploy, but no one believed me. My business dealings dried up and I found myself working here."

"When did this happen?"

"Two years ago."

Ehrich stiffened. He recalled his arrival in this dimension and the horses he had spooked. Could he have been responsible for this? He dismissed the coincidence "Sir, is there anything we can do to get those investors back?"

"I appreciate your offer, young man, but I'm going to have to start at the beginning. Thank you though for exposing the spy."

"I wish I could have done more."

Tesla shook himself out of his daze. "You may have cast doubt in the investors' minds. Perhaps they will be as reluctant to go with Edison as they are to go with me. That is a small victory."

"Do you think they may change their minds?" Ehrich asked.

The thin scientist laughed. "If there's anything I've learned about doing business in this country, it is that, when it comes to making money, no deal is ever truly dead. Let's not dwell on today's events. I need to distract myself with something positive. You wanted to learn about the book, didn't you?"

"Commander Farrier will be pleased you have some information."

"Ehrich, stop pretending. The commander is not interested in this book. You are."

"What? No. I swear—the commander wants to know."

"You will have to learn to lie better. The commander only cares about weapons and the book is far from a weapon. Why do you want to learn about this book?"

Ehrich sighed. "It's complicated, sir."

"So is the device, but I was able to unlock some of its secrets. The only thing I could not learn was why you care."

Ehrich eyed the thin man and weighed his options. Perhaps he could tell him only what he needed to know. "You see the insignia on the spine?"

Tesla nodded. Ehrich pulled his medallion by the leather strap and showed him the same image. "I'm wondering what the connection is. I picked this up from a Dimensional," he said. Technically, he was telling the truth.

Tesla examined the gears within the medallion's two loops. The gear wheels of the main loops could turn, making a distinct click with each turn, but the movement caused nothing to happen.

"Who did you get the medallion from? Maybe you could ask them."

"That's the problem. My brother was wearing it moments before—" Ehrich shook his head. "I don't know where he got it from. I'd never seen it before."

"What happened to him?"

Ehrich looked down. "It was my job to look after Dash. Mother told me to keep an eye out for him," Ehrich said. "But I failed and he died."

"I'm sorry. How did it happen?"

For so long he had kept all his pain bottled inside. He wanted to confess everything. He pictured the look on Dash's face right before his brother ran into the knife. His eyes were cold and accusing, but Ehrich couldn't bring himself to tell Tesla. He wasn't ready.

Tesla patted him on the shoulder. "My brother died many years ago. He was on his way back to my father's farm. He was on the path back to the house when he fell off his horse and hit his head. He never woke up again. It was a terrible accident. I miss my brother every day."

"I'm sorry to hear that, Mr. Tesla."

"We are united in spirit, Ehrich. We've both lost someone we have loved."

Ehrich nodded. He felt comfortable with Tesla in a way he had never felt around Charlie or the other squad mates. Tesla lived on this island, separate from the people on Devil's Island; he even separated himself from the workers on Randall's Island, hiding in his ivory tower. While he was no Dimensional, he was an outsider to Demon Watch, and from what Ehrich could see, pretty much everyone else. Yet, what was intriguing about the man's isolation was that he seemed not only to acknowledge it but to embrace it.

"I don't know if Dash stole the medallion from a Dimensional or if someone gave it to him moments before he died. What I'm sure of is that this medallion and his death are connected somehow."

"How old was your brother?"

"Ten."

"A curious age," Tesla said, stroking his moustache. "He could have picked the medallion up off the street."

"I don't think so, but I need to know. If I can get some answers, maybe I can make sense of what happened to him."

"Then let us begin our search," Tesla said. He ran his finger along the spine and pressed the insignia. The book cover popped open, revealing gears and cogs within the thick tome. From the innards rose a carousel with cut-out images around the black surface. A light shone through the shapes and formed silhouettes on the wall. The carousel began to turn, slowly at first but quickly gathering speed.

The image of a jade tael, a circular disk with a square hole in the centre, formed before their eyes. Indecipherable symbols were etched around the square, wrapping around the circle.

A girl's voice spoke over the image. "This jade tael belongs to the House of Qi. Let the tael be a symbol of our alliance. When you see it, you can trust whatever comes after."

The image of a ruby-skinned amazon girl appeared in place of the jade tael. Her black hair was braided into a long ponytail and her eyes were a deep magenta. Two small ivory tusks protruded from either side of her nose. She wore a sleeveless green robe that revealed leather armlets around powerful biceps. A jade tael hung on a leather strap around her neck.

"Who is that?" Ehrich asked.

Tesla shook his head. "Another mystery to be solved."

The red-skinned girl spoke again. "Contact me after your engineers have examined this. I'm certain you will be interested in what I have to say."

Her image faded out, replaced with a technical blueprint of what appeared to be a metal arm. At the elbow, there was a set of servos and gears that operated cables connected to the hand. The schematic blinked out and the carousel stopped rotating.

"Now you know the purpose of the device," Tesla said. "Although it doesn't use pages, it does contain information; from what I could see, information related to this Dimensional. If you find her, you'll find the connection to the insignia."

Ehrich chewed his bottom lip, wondering why Amina needed to ally herself with the red-skinned girl. The mechanical plans suggested their alliance had something to do with technology. What bothered Ehrich was that he didn't know why they needed this technology.

THE MEMORY CLOUD

Over the next two days, Ehrich had found himself stretched thin. Between working for Tesla and helping the squad with their administrative punishment, he barely had time to search for Amina. Today, he caught a break. The squad had no graves to dig and Tesla had no tasks for him. Ehrich could focus on the search.

The newcomers' quarantine area reminded Ehrich of the Bowery where the street urchins slept in alleyways. As he walked through the women's section, the curious Dimensionals whispered quietly. Some stared at Ehrich. Others just gazed blankly at the walls. Their glassy eyes made him think of Jacob Riis' newspaper photos of Lower East Side tenement dwellers. They looked through him as if they were trying to peer beyond him—beyond the walls themselves.

He stopped near an empty bed where one occupant had scrawled on the wall:

Buried alive under their rules,
Life teems around, but not for me.
Let me hear robins greet the morn,
What is life if it is not lived free?

Ehrich knew the answer as soon as he read the question. It was the life he had been living for the last two years, essentially a prisoner of this dimension. Though he could move freely through the city, he could never be free to be himself. He was a Dimensional like the ones stuck here. The only difference was that no one had figured out his secret, and he had to keep it this way, at least until he found the truth about his brother. He was sure that Amina held the key to the end of the quest—if he could just find her.

Only two days had passed since Amina's arrival on Devil's Island, so Ehrich assumed that she would still be in quarantine. He described the girl to the newcomers in quarantine, but few spoke English, and those who did speak English did not want to speak to him. He even investigated the children's dormitory in case Amina had been sent there. No sign of her anywhere.

Then he remembered Piotravisk, the Dimensional who claimed the same sponsor as Amina. Ehrich headed to the men's quarantine area and found the old man on a cot far away from the others. Piotravisk swirled his hands in the air. White wisps of smoke appeared and morphed into images of the man's home world. Ehrich had never seen a more elegant illusion; magicians would kill to be able to recreate such a feat.

The green-skinned man seemed oblivious to his surroundings as he conjured images of pyramids and a never-ending seascape, all from his perspective. The memory cloud turned to a field littered with bodies covered in black blood. Ehrich leaned closer and saw round razor-sharp discs littered across the ground. These silver taels had square holes in the centre like the jade tael the red-skinned girl wore. However, these taels were used as weapons to slaughter Piotravisk's race.

"What happened to your people?" Ehrich asked.

The images disappeared along with the smoke as the man clasped his hands together. He said nothing.

"You were attacked. Who did it?" Ehrich asked.

Piotravisk shook his head.

"Do you understand what I'm saying?"

"My friend. You see her? My name Piotravisk. Her name Amina."

Ehrich's eyes lit up. "Can you show me your friend? How do you know her?"

Piotravisk opened his hands. Smoke rose from his fingertips as the illusion of his world appeared once more. Ehrich examined the images of the fallen bodies and the metal taels strewn across the scorched earth. Making her way through the carnage was the dark-skinned Dimensional he sought. She held her hand out and said, "Sir, the army has destroyed everything. You can't stay here any more."

Ehrich leaned forward. Piotravisk's voice drifted up from the memory cloud. "Who are you?" it asked.

"A friend."

"Will you help me find my wife?'

Amina pursed her lips and answered, "Sure, sure. We'll look for survivors. But it's not safe here. We have to leave the area."

"Why?" Piotravisk's voice asked.

A shrill whistle. The memory cloud shifted perspective to reveal the source of the sound. A shadowy figure hopped across the battlefield. The figure bent over a fallen person's head and picked up an orb with his metal glove. He glanced up at Amina, and his eyes widened with recognition.

He curled the metal talons of his gloved hand and hissed, "Pes-s-st."

Piotravisk spat on the dormitory floor. "*Maturator du straeda*," he said in his own language before trying to translate for Ehrich. "Rat… Scavenger."

In the memory cloud, Amina raised a crossbow and took aim, but the figure scurried away. Ehrich had seen this scavenger before. He was Ole Lukoje, the raggedy man.

MR. SANDMAN RETURNS

In Dante's *Inferno,* the Ninth Circle of Hell was reserved for traitors: Cain and Judas were frozen in a lake along with Mordred, the man who betrayed King Arthur. On Devil's Island, the Ninth Circle was reserved for those who broke the laws of the land when they tried to smuggle themselves into New York. Their crime was one of desperation.

What spurred such desperation? Piotravisk's memory cloud offered a glimpse of the bleak worlds the Dimensionals fled. Ehrich only wished the old man knew more about his rescuer, Amina, but Piotravisk only knew her as his saviour. The way Ole Lukoje reacted to Amina, Ehrich suspected the two might have a prior relationship, albeit an unfriendly one. At this point, any connection to Amina was a lead that Ehrich had to follow.

The temperature rose as the lift descended into the depths. The engineers had dynamited a remote part of the island, away from Demon Gate and the dormitories, to fashion the prison beneath the surface, but they failed to install proper ventilation. The only way to reach Ninth Circle was through the wire mesh lift. Escape was virtually impossible, even for the hot and stale air.

Two burly Devil's Island guards eyed Ehrich warily as the lift came to a stop at the bottom. They recognized his duster as the hunter's uniform and let him pass. He crossed the vast, man-made cavern. The arc lamps lining the pathway to the guardhouse at the far end lit up the rocky walls and stalactites overhead. A family of bats hung from a few of the outcroppings. The ground level was uneven but clear of obstructions. Beside the mouth of a tunnel, a funicular sat on tracks that led into a dark tunnel. This cable car transport was the only way down to the prison cells, protected by the half dozen teens milling about the guardhouse.

A redhead chewing on the end of a chicken bone strutted over to Ehrich.

"Bit late for a visit, isn't it?" He spit out the bone and reached into his vest pocket to pull out his stem-winder. He popped the cover with a flourish and checked the time. "I thought hunters kept banker's hours."

The onlookers chuckled.

"I'm here to interrogate one of the prisoners," Ehrich said.

"Bully for you. Where's your paperwork?"

"I've never needed any before."

"Well, shine my shoes. That's because you came during *regular* hours, but since you're here *after* hours, I'm going to need to see some *paperwork*. You're welcome to come back tomorrow during *regular* hours, but if you want to go down the hole now, I need the right *paperwork*."

"Forget this nonsense." Ehrich stepped toward the funicular. The redhead blocked his way.

"Like I said—you produce the *paperwork*, I'll let you go down and do whatever you want for however long you want to do it."

The freckled boy's attempt at a shakedown was as obvious as his unruly mop of red hair. Even if Ehrich had the extortionist's money, he wouldn't pay. Instead, he asked, "What's your name?"

"Brian. Why? You plan to report me to Commander Farrier? Go ahead. Might as well be throwing water in the Mississippi."

"No," Ehrich said. "Did you hear what happened to one of the hunters?"

Brian said nothing, but one of the teens behind him piped up, "I heard someone had a run in. Had half their face torn off."

A cross-eyed teen shook her head. "No, a demon bit his head clean off."

The others added bits and pieces of gossip. Stories had a way of distorting when they were passed down the grapevine, and Ehrich used this to his advantage.

"Never saw anything like it. It wasn't so much *that* Louis died; it was more *how* he died."

Brian sneered. "You know the risks when you take the job."

His comrades agreed.

Ehrich shook his head. "Thing is, Brian, the illegal reanimated a dead woman to do his dirty work. The woman drove a pipe into Louis' stomach. He suffered right until the end."

The guards fell silent.

"The illegal who did this wasn't alone," Ehrich lied. "We think there are at least seven others roaming New York. We're thinking we need some bait to lure them out, and my squad leader needs a volunteer."

Ehrich fixed a steady gaze at Brian, who blanched, but didn't budge from his position. He wasn't about to lose face.

Ehrich smiled and nodded at the cross-eyed guard. "What's your name?"

She shrank back. The others stared at their boots.

"Well, *Brian,* I'm sure I could lose your name as easily as you lose your need for *paperwork*."

The young man glared at Ehrich. "Don't break your neck climbing into the hole." He nodded to one of the teens, who jogged into the guardhouse.

Ehrich strolled to the funicular and climbed on the platform. He perched on the giant angled risers of the cable car. "You've been a great help, Brian."

Brian glared at him as the funicular jerked forward on the tracks and slowly rolled into the tunnel. The funicular angled so that Ehrich was now sitting upright on the platform's tiered risers. Harsh gaslights lined the tracks, illuminating the long descent into the prison area. After what seemed like an eternity, the cart reached the bottom. He stepped off and headed through the prison's corridors. Each cell was lined with the fine-wire mesh used in Faraday Cages. The mesh nullified any devices that relied on energy. In addition, the walls were reinforced with iron bars thick enough to withstand dynamite blasts. Most of the illegals in the cells were desperate newcomers trying to find a new life in this dimension, but a few were what Farrier called class-nine Dimensionals: beings with malicious intent or abilities considered dangerous to the citizens of New York. The engineers had constructed the cells with these types of prisoners in mind. Each spartan cell had a cot to sleep on, a bucket for filth, and a tray for food. The prisoners glared at Ehrich as he passed.

He slowed when he reached his destination. The glow from the arc lanterns affixed to the stone walls shed enough light for him to see Ole Lukoje perched on a hard cot inside his dank cell. A filth bucket sat near the bars and the sharp reek punched up Ehrich's nose. The raggedy man hissed as soon as he noticed the husky, brown-haired teen, but he looked less intimidating minus his metal gloves and dust-laden overcoat.

"Have you come back for my other arm, fles-s-sh bag?" Ole Lukoje hissed.

"I need some information."

"Then you have come to the wrong plac-c-c-e."

"I know what you do, Ole Lukoje. You're a parasite looking for hosts and when you run out, you move on. I have seen where you've been, and I know that angry people want to get their hands on you. I might let them know where to find you."

The raggedy man said nothing. His nose whistled as he breathed.

"Now, I could be persuaded not to share your location if you were to share some information with me," Ehrich said.

"What do you wis-s-sh to know?" Ole Lukoje asked.

"You visited a dimension where green-skinned people lived. Remember?"

"Those fles-s-sh bags had already given up their lives-s-s when I took their peepers-s-s. You can't hold me res-s-spons-s-sible for that. No one can."

"You saw a dark-skinned girl with an old man. She tried to shoot you with a crossbow. Who was she?"

"Ah, yes-s-s. Her kind likes-s-s to pick up s-s-strays-s-s."

"What do you mean?" Ehrich asked.

"All thos-s-se people already dead. S-s-so few s-s-strays-s-s to s-s-save."

"Stop playing games."

Ole Lukoje drifted deeper into his cell. "A total was-s-ste. Dead peepers-s-s are s-s-stale and dry."

"Are you going to tell me or not?"

"Free me and I will tell you all you need to know." The raggedy man leaned back on his cot, his nose whistling. "No? What a s-s-shame."

A dead end. Ehrich sighed and walked away from the cell, lost in thought. He turned a corner and took a few steps before realizing he had gone the wrong way. As he came back around the corner, he saw a prisoner that stopped him in his tracks.

A giant crimson-skinned creature with black, braided hair rose to his feet and approached the barred door of his cell. Two tusks extended from either side of the giant's flared nose. He wore black trousers and an emerald vest that was open to reveal his developed chest and abdomen. Hanging around the creature's neck on a leather strap was a jade tael, just like the one from Amina's device. Indecipherable symbols were etched around the square hole of the thick green ring. The prisoner looked like the girl on the device, right down to the magenta eyes, black ponytail-styled queue and the tusks protruding from either side of his nose.

"I have a complaint about the quality of the food you have been serving." The red-skinned man spoke in precise, formal English but with an exotic, drawling accent.

"I am s-s-surpris-s-ed at you, Ba Tian. S-s-speaking to a Hunter like that. Tissk tissk!"

Ba Tian scowled at Ole Lukoje, and the raggedy man fell silent.

Ehrich stepped to the red-skinned prisoner's cell door. "Why are you here, Ba Tian?"

"I'm a humble merchant trying to peddle my wares."

"If you were that, you wouldn't be here. Ninth Circle is for the illegals."

"This arrest is a misunderstanding. I had goods that needed to be shipped here immediately and your bureaucratic protocols would have had my shipment tied up for months. I was attempting to expedite the delivery for my client. I will gladly pay the fine or whatever I must do to be returned to my world."

Ehrich feigned a smile, trying to get on the prisoner's good side. He gestured to the jade tael necklace around the man's neck. "Interesting amulet you have there. I think I've seen it before."

The red-skinned prisoner raised an eyebrow. "Oh? Where?"

"Must have been on one of the Dimensionals who came through legal means. Those markings are interesting. What do they mean?"

The crimson man held up the tael. "In my people's language, it is our credo. *Death before dishonour.*"

"I didn't realize exporting was a deadly business," Ehrich said.

Ba Tian's eyes flashed anger, but he smiled. "Yes, we are a serious people."

"Are there many peddlers like yourself?" Ehrich probed.

The man shook his head. "Tell me where you saw the other tael. Perhaps it is a fellow citizen who can vouch for me."

Ehrich shrugged. "I can't seem to recall exactly where I saw her, but I know she had cleared immigration. Maybe there's a place in America that your peddlers are told to go when they arrive."

"I go where the money is," Ba Tian said, stone-faced. "Unfortunately, your people are an insecure lot. You are happy to buy wares from my kind when the goods are cheaper than your own merchants,' but as soon as you make the purchase, you want us banished from your sight. Your people value the wares more than the relationship, but you don't understand they are linked."

"What is it that you sell, Ba Tian?"

The red-skinned man smiled. "Ice. I understand that your people are fond of keeping things cold. But if you have any particular desires, I've travelled to many places and have contacts everywhere."

"In your travels have you come across many symbols? Flags? Crests?"

"Many. Are you looking for anything in particular?"

Ehrich looked over his shoulder. They were alone. He reached for the medallion under his shirt. His fingers hooked around the metal gears. Dash's voice flashed in his mind like the imprint of a fading nightmare: "*Ehrich...No*!"

Ehrich shut out the accusation. "Are you familiar with this?" he asked the prisoner.

The Dimensional's eyes narrowed when he examined the medallion dangling from Ehrich's hand. He took in a sharp, short breath when he saw the chimera on the back cover.

"Well?" Ehrich asked.

“First of all, the crest is of a proud people from the Vena system,” Ba Tian said.

“Who are they?”

The red-skinned man cracked a thin-lipped smile. “Information is currency. What will you give in exchange for what you seek?”

“You said you wanted to be deported. I might be able to make that happen,” Ehrich lied.

Ba Tian smiled. “Can I take another look at the medallion?”

Ehrich held it up by the strap. “Who are the people of Vena?”

“They are dust,” the crimson man laughed.

The Dimensional knew more, but he wasn’t about to tell Ehrich without something in return. Unfortunately, Ehrich had nothing to offer.

The boy stuffed the medallion under his shirt. “I’ll remember your helpfulness to the commander.”

Ba Tian stopped chortling. “Wait, wait. Tell your commander, whatever the fine, I’ll pay. As long as I can be sent back to my own dimension.” He plucked his jade tael from around his neck. “This tael is worth more than any of your precious metals combined. It could mark the beginning of a fruitful relationship.”

Ehrich ignored the offer and walked away from the cell. Thoughts swirled around his mind. Was the medallion’s original owner from Vena? He had to go back to his only real lead—Amina’s book.

TESLA IN TROUBLE

Ehrich crossed the bridge that spanned the two islands and ran to Tesla's tower. By now, he was a familiar enough sight that the guards didn't stop him as he pushed through the doors and bounded up the stairs to tell Tesla about his first lead.

He headed to the upper levels to search the labs for Tesla. The first lab was filled with copper wires, stators, iron tubes, gears, and various other items that would make an engineer giddy. A second lab looked like a zoo of mechanical animals. The coils of copper wire looked more like a snake aquarium, and the giant machines with gear heads were like trophy heads from a safari. Ehrich wasn't sure if these were confiscated devices or Tesla's own inventions.

When he reached Tesla's AC coil demonstration lab, he was stunned to see the room's condition. Someone had ransacked the place. Equipment was broken and scattered, and the coil towers had been knocked down.

He leapt up the stairs three at a time until he arrived at the top level where he heard a shout. Through a set of double doors, there came the crackling sound of electricity. Ehrich followed the sound and flung the doors open.

There, in the centre of a trio of electrical towers, a disheveled Tesla stood with his arms raised. The doughnut-shaped rings at the top of the narrow towers discharged electricity which the scientist caught in his thick, mesh-gloved hands. Then he hurled a blue sizzling ball at a figure at the corner of the room.

Amina! She rolled out of the way of the lightning ball and it seared the wall behind her.

"I want my Codex back!" she demanded.

"I would not come any closer," Tesla warned. "You will regret it."

Amina crouched low, tensing as if to spring. The scientist summoned the electricity from his coils and hurled ball after ball of energy at the girl. She dodged them deftly, rolling across the floor and moving closer to Tesla until she was nearly on top of him. He threw one last ball of energy at her, but only succeeded in charring the marble floor. Amina dove across the floor and picked up the book device at Tesla's feet. Then with a leg sweep, she knocked him down and sprinted to the doorway where Ehrich blocked her exit.

Amina launched herself into the air and fell on him with her full weight. He rolled as soon as he hit the floor, pushing his feet against her belly and flipping her over. She landed with catlike grace. He sprang up and spun to grab Amina before she could turn around, but she unleashed a mule kick at Ehrich's chest. He staggered back into the room.

Tesla extended his hand to summon more electricity from the towers, but Amina picked up the heavy cable on the floor and yanked it out of the base of the crackling tower. The loose end sparked with deadly energy as she advanced. Ehrich stepped in front of Tesla to protect him from the brunt of the attack, but Amina did not deliver a killing blow. Instead, she threw the cable at the window. Cold air rushed into the room. Ehrich turned in time to see the girl dive out the open window. He rushed to the ledge and poked his head out. She was gone. Far below, there was no body on the ground. It was as if she had vanished.

In the distance, the lone caw of a seagull echoed over the water.

HUNTER NO MORE

The battle had left the lab in ruins, but that was nothing compared to what its aftermath did to George Farrier's temper. While Devil's Island guards combed the room for clues to help them track Amina, Farrier limped toward Ehrich, the wood of his peg leg thudding on the marble floor.

"Explain to me exactly what happened."

"A Dimensional escaped from Devil's Island and came here to retrieve a device we had confiscated from her."

"Impossible. No one can leave my facilities without my guards knowing it. She must have come from outside the island."

"Commander, I recognized her as one of the new arrivals."

"My security is airtight. No one gets out of there without my knowing."

"I don't know how she slipped out, sir, but she did." Ehrich couldn't believe that the commander was being so thick-headed.

"No, Mr. Weisz. There is no way anyone could have left."

"Sir, I think she's meeting someone here."

"Tarnation. A Dimensional breaks out of my facility just so she can meet someone," Farrier said. "Aren't you the wellspring of useless observations?"

Tesla interrupted, "I believe she is looking for a red-skinned girl. This second girl has interesting taste in jewellery, including a jade coin with a square in the centre. You wouldn't be able to miss her. She has tusks on either side of her nose."

The commander asked, "How do you know all this?"

"I examined the Dimensional's device, and it brought up the image of a red-skinned girl."

"Tarnation. Now I have to look for two Dimensionals instead of one." He turned to the guards. "Search this island and find the fugitive. We have ourselves a bug hunt."

"Commander, I'd like to join the search."

"No, you're still on administrative duty, and I don't think that was supposed to include running out to this island. You want to tell me why you were here in the first place?"

"He is working for me," Tesla explained.

"Well, shut my mouth. Mr. Tesla, in all our time together, I've never once seen you ask for help from anyone."

"Mr. Weisz brought me the item belonging to the fugitive to examine, and he has been providing a valuable service ever since. I would like him to continue."

"I'd like my right foot back, but that's not going to happen any time soon."

"Mr. Farrier, if not for this young lad, the damage could have been much worse. Can you imagine the Demon Watch without weapons? I believe I will need to conduct a thorough test of the arsenal now to assess the damage and make sure she didn't tamper with anything before I caught her in my lab. It might be weeks, even months before you receive any new weapons. My work would go much faster if I had help."

Farrier glowered but said nothing.

"I'm in this boy's debt. Without him, I'm sure I would be dead right now."

"Mr. Tesla, I can post more guards at your research facilities."

"The same ones who allowed the woman to escape your island, Mr. Farrier? No, I'll keep my own security, thank you." He turned to Ehrich. "Young man, I am promoting you to my personal bodyguard."

"Absolutely not. I forbid it," Farrier said. "He is under my command."

"Not any more. He transferred to my facilities as an apprentice, and I'm loathe to lose him."

Farrier rubbed his salt and pepper beard, eyeing Ehrich. Finally, he spoke. "Good riddance. You are no longer a hunter, Ehrich Weisz." He hobbled out of the lab, moving swiftly on his peg leg.

When they were alone, Ehrich found he could breathe again. "Thank you."

"Don't thank me yet. There's a mess to clean up."

"Me? I thought I was your security."

"Yes, you are, and the next time my lab is attacked by an inter-dimensional being, I fully expect you to be there to defend me."

"Mr. Tesla, I think the attack may be coming sooner than you think. I have to find Amina before she can come at you again."

"Or is it because she may have answers to your questions?"

"Either way, we need to catch her," Ehrich said.

Tesla nodded. "Come with me."

The scientist led Ehrich to another room that contained an array of devices in various stages of completion. They were prototype weapons. The tables littered with coils, gears, and metal parts reminded Ehrich of the Mary Shelley novel, *Frankenstein*. What kind of monsters was Tesla creating?

Tesla counted his steps to a nearby lab table and began rummaging through the materials. On the table sat a strange box of gears, cogs, and doughnut-shaped toroids. For a moment, Ehrich was reminded of his childhood. His father had taken Dash and him to attend the show of a touring magician, an old friend of his father's. The magician had made an orange tree grow in a clay pot before the audience's eyes. Ehrich's mouth dropped as he watched leaves sprout instantly on the branches, and he was the lucky recipient of the orange the magician had plucked from the tiny tree.

When they went backstage, Ehrich snuck away and examined the clay pot. He understood the magician would never reveal the secret of the tree, but he had to see for himself how it worked. He was able to pry off the back cover, revealing an intricate mechanism that whirred and pushed out fake leaves on the branches.

Here, in Tesla's lab, the device before him seemed similar, but instead of the internal works pushing oranges out, they controlled six toroids. Ehrich recalled how the oranges were driven by a central gear mechanism. He reached into the mechanism and played with one of the gears. The cog slid down the bar. Ehrich tried to pull it back up. He was great at theory, lousy at practise.

Tesla glanced up. “No, no, no. Don’t touch that. Careful.”

Ehrich pulled back his hand. “Sorry, sir. I just thought I might have seen this design before.”

“Not possible. This is my original creation.”

“I’m sure I’ve seen this mechanism before. Is it meant to push these coils out?”

The man stroked the high cheekbones of his face and smiled. “Yes, how did you know?”

“The gears are connected to the centre rotating bar. I imagined they had to power something, but there is no engine, only these coils.”

Tesla looked as delighted as Dash did when the magician produced the oranges. “Toroids, not coils, but you are correct.”

“What are the coils, I mean *toroids*, supposed to do?” Ehrich asked.

Now it was the scientist’s turn to create some magic. He flicked a switch on the box. The toroids crackled with electricity. Ehrich stepped back quickly, but his companion was nonplussed.

“One... two... three... One...” Tesla counted as he made his way to another station where a prototype pistol was mounted. The weapon looked like a volt pistol without the electro-dart chamber. Instead, an antenna protruded from the top of the barrel.

He aimed the gun at a clothes-dummy target standing amid the remains of other targets. A sizzling bolt of blue energy shot across the room and struck the target.

Tesla smiled, “The world’s first wireless electric generator. The range is about twenty feet. Not enough to revolutionize the world, but enough for a squad of hunters in a firefight.”

"Is that what you wanted to show me?"

"No. If you are going up against dangerous illegals, you might need to be equipped with more than just your wits. Ah, here." Tesla picked up a volt pistol which also lacked an electro-dart chamber.

"Where are the electro-darts?" Ehrich asked. "Am I supposed to lug the generator with me?"

"No darts and no generator. You can fire ten times before the pistol requires recharging. Give it five minutes and you'll have another round of five. Let it sit for an hour, you'll have full power."

"And what happens when I run out of power?"

Tesla smiled and gripped the barrel of the pistol like a makeshift club. "Any device can be turned into a weapon, when you are desperate."

Ehrich smiled. "Thank you, sir. Should I organize the island guards to help search the grounds and labs?"

Tesla shook his head. "If the Dimensional had the means to slip out of Demon Gate and get on this island, I have little doubt that she would have used those same means to spirit herself away."

"Then we're going to have to look for where she might go," Ehrich said.

"And do you have an idea of where?"

"Her sponsor's," Ehrich answered.

MUSEUM OF CURIOSITIES

The day after the attack on Tesla's lab, Ehrich travelled to Manhattan to begin his search for Amina. It hadn't taken long for him to find her sponsor's place of business. Dime museums tended to be located in the Bowery. It only took asking a newsie or two to locate the building, which was in the shadow of the Third Avenue elevated railroad.

The sign on the Bowery establishment promised some kind of scientific enlightenment, but the Museum of Curiosities was more sideshow than education. The rundown three-story building rivalled even the seediest of Bowery businesses in dilapidation. Inside its principal showroom, various display cases held curious abnormalities. Ehrich leaned closer to examine a mummified fish with the head of a howling infant. Beside the case was a table of petrified bugs. The fossilized insects ranged from giant millipedes with moth wings, to spiders with crab claws, to a cockroach with three heads.

A rustling caught his attention. Ehrich sensed someone was watching him through the red curtain of the doorway behind the counter.

"Hello? Anyone here?" he asked.

The curtain parted and a German shepherd padded out, growling. Ehrich stood his ground. The dog's hackles raised as it bared its teeth.

"Easy, there. I don't mean to hurt you. Just wanted to look around."

A meaty hand snaked through the curtain and waved at the dog. "It's all right."

The dog stopped growling as the rest of a giant man emerged. Ehrich thought that he was a bit of a curiosity himself: The buttons on his striped shirt threatened to pop off and take out an eye. The tufts of purple hair that sprouted above his ears almost seemed to have a mind of their own, waving around every time the man shook his head or spoke. He peeked over his silver-rimmed spectacles at Ehrich.

"Ah, you've come to see the marvelous curiosities nature produces. Well, behind the curtain are wonders no man or woman has ever seen elsewhere. And you'll never see their ilk ever again. All it will cost you is a shiny little dime."

"Actually, I'm not interested."

"They always begin as sceptics, but they always leave as believers. Let me give you a taste, son." He clapped his hands.

A few seconds later, a woman's leg cut through the slit of the curtain. Ehrich's gaze wandered up the fishnet stockings to the emerging tight, red corset that hugged her slender torso. Then a black-gloved hand and arm, a bare shoulder, until—Ehrich's eyes nearly popped out of his head. The woman sported a lumberjack's beard. Golden hair cascaded down her back, but all Ehrich could do was gape at the cobalt-blue beard which wriggled on the woman's face. On closer inspection, he realized that the facial hair was actually a mass of writhing blue caterpillars.

"No doubt, you can see a bearded lady at any museum, but no one has ever seen one like this, and that is just a fraction of what lies behind the curtain. One shiny little dime for the wonders of the world. What do you say?"

"I'm not sure if you have what I'm looking for. Are you Mr. Serenity?"

"Indeed I am. So my reputation precedes me—I'm flattered. How did you hear of me?"

"Word on the street is that you have attractions that no one else does."

"Son, if I don't have it here, no one does."

"I'm interested in a girl," Ehrich said.

The bearded lady wiggled her corset down an inch. "Women are much more interesting."

Ehrich smiled. "I'm sure you are, but I need to find this girl."

Mr. Serenity narrowed his gaze and waved the bearded lady to the back. "There is a brothel two blocks over."

"No. You misunderstand. This girl has information I need. I was told she might be here."

"May I ask why this girl is so important?"

"Isn't this the Museum of Curiosities? I'm here to satisfy mine."

The man's jowls rippled as he shook his head. "Look elsewhere." He stepped around the counter with the German shepherd at his side.

“Okay, but if the girl should happen to show up, let her know I have this.” He thrust his hand into his shirt and pulled out Dash’s medallion by the strap.

“Does this image mean anything to you?” Ehrich asked.

Mr. Serenity blinked once. “Never seen it before.”

“Any idea what it might mean?”

The dog barked, cutting into the silence.

“You know what, son? I have some books in the back. I might be able to find some information to help you. Wait here.” Mr. Serenity lumbered behind the counter and through the curtain. The German shepherd eyed Ehrich, then followed its master into the back.

Ehrich paced around the cramped lobby, examining the other curios in the shop. Many of them appeared to be obvious fakes. Was Mr. Serenity merely a shill posing as a sponsor for a quick buck or two? Time seemed to pass forever, and Ehrich began to fidget. Had the old man run off on him? He finally decided to investigate.

Beyond the curtains was a narrow hallway bracketed on both sides by a series of surprisingly large display areas. The first two areas were unoccupied. In the third, the bearded lady reclined on a divan. Opposite her was a thick-necked giant with talons for hands perched on a trapeze. Ehrich nodded at him.

In another space, two women were conjoined at the hip with a scorpion tail rising from their back. Next to them was a morbidly obese man with octopus tentacles for arms.

He found a set of stairs at the far end of the hall, and followed past the sleeping quarters on the second floor to the offices on the top floor. Down the hall, Mr. Serenity stepped out of a doorway. “Impatient, aren’t we? I think I’ve found something.”

He held up a book and beckoned Ehrich over.

"Come in, son. This is truly remarkable."

"What is it?"

"I'll show you in my office. *Après vous,* as the French people of your dimension say."

Mr. Serenity's tiny office contained a roll-top desk littered with papers and a bookshelf bursting with dusty tomes. Ehrich stepped over a pile of books. Something didn't seem right about the office. For an instant, the desk flickered like a mirage and the perspective seemed off. How could the desk be so far away in such a tiny space?

"I think I've seen enough," Ehrich said, and turned around.

A barred door slammed in his face. He pulled on it but it held fast. When he turned around again, the office was gone, replaced with an empty cell.

"You're going nowhere, boy," Mr. Serenity said.

THINGS HEAT UP

Ehrich drew his volt pistol. "Open the door now."

Mr. Serenity laughed and shook his head. "Go ahead and shoot."

Ehrich pulled the trigger. Electrical energy flew from the doughnut-shaped end of the barrel and lit up the bars of the cell door, but dissipated quickly. Mr. Serenity grabbed the bars of the cell door and smiled. Ehrich fired at the man, but the door absorbed the energy. Mr. Serenity didn't even flinch as the electricity danced around his fingers. He drew a small crossbow pistol from behind his back. The bowstring was taut, holding a cruel barbed dart, and ready to fire.

"A remarkable cell, don't you think? Loves to absorb energy, but ignores physical projectiles. Now put the gun on the floor and kick it out."

Ehrich considered Tesla's suggestion that any device could be turned into a weapon, but he wasn't desperate enough yet.

He needed answers more than he needed to fight. He placed the pistol on the wooden floor and kicked it through the bars.

"You wait right there while we figure out what to do with you." Mr. Serenity picked up the weapon and walked away.

Ehrich tested the bars of the door, which was solidly locked. He examined the room for any other exit, but found none except for a small window—far too small for him to squeeze through. Even if he could climb out, the ground was three floors down. A heated discussion in the next room attracted his attention.

"I say we kill him," a gruff man said.

Mr. Serenity answered, "No, he's a member of the Demon Watch. If he dies, they'll come after us."

"They'll come for us anyway if we let him go."

"I don't think so. He wasn't with the others. Why did he come here by himself?"

"Someone check the street. There might be others spying on us."

A woman's voice cut through the chatter. "Enough. If they're going to look for him, the best thing to do is not be here when they find him."

Mr. Serenity disagreed. "We told the asset to find us here. We can't abandon the post."

"I say we hold the hunter until the meeting," she said.

"Then what?" Mr. Serenity asked, his voice lowering.

"Then he's a liability."

Mutters of agreement. He stepped back from the cell door. Was Amina the asset? Or was it the red-skinned girl? What was her connection to this collection of freaks? And what was so significant about her book? He could wait in the cell until she showed up so he could ask her the questions, but he didn't know what the Dimensionals would do to him after she arrived.

He needed to get out.

He knelt down and cracked open the false heel on his right shoe to retrieve his lock-pick set. Then he reached through the bars around to the keyhole. He slipped the hook pick into the keyhole and carefully slid it around, feeling for the tumbler, hoping to catch one of the lock's pins. No luck on the first try. Again. No success. Once more. Nothing.

A few dozen failures later, Ehrich began to doubt himself. He knew that he couldn't perform under the pressure of being watched, but when no one was looking, he could usually pick any lock. Now, a different kind of pressure was making his hands tremble. He wiped the sweat off on his wool trousers and inserted the pick into the lock with a growing sense of impatience. He jammed the instrument, lodging the pick in the lock mechanism. After several minutes, he was unable to pull his hook pick free. He punched the cell door.

"Sakes alive!" he nursed his sore knuckles.

Once he recovered, he ran his hand along the rough wood walls, hoping to find another way to escape. On a shelf above the door, a "Cyclops" eye on a copper box stared at him. He cocked his head to the side and scratched his head. Why hadn't he seen this before? He climbed the bars and pulled down the device. No wires were connected to the machine, but inside the mechanism was a metal spindle that operated a series of tiny gears which spun a carousel, like the one in Amina's book. In the middle of the unit was a tiny light bulb and what looked to be a strange tiny photograph. When he examined the stamp-sized, translucent picture, he saw Mr. Serenity's office. The lens magnified and projected the image over the cell walls. He had fallen for an illusion. He needed to be more careful in the future about taking things at face value.

Nikola Tesla's advice rang in Ehrich's ears. *If you want to convince people of something, you have to give them a show. Give them the illusion of what you want them to see so you can get what you really wan*t. Ehrich needed his own illusion, and he knew just how to make it.

Ehrich leaned the device against the wall and pulled apart the innards. He yanked out the spindle and removed the gears to give him some space. Then he used his tension wrench to lever the lens from its housing. He tore strips from the bottom of his shirt and piled them on the floor near the wall, where the sunlight was hitting. He used his tension wrench again to scrape wood shavings off the floor and piled them on top of the cloth strips. Then he knelt to the side, focussing the sun through the lens at the kindling. He stayed as still as he could, resting his elbow on his knee, keeping the lens over the pile of wood shavings. Time inched along as slowly as the bead of perspiration now starting to roll down Ehrich's temple. His hand ached, but he refused to shift position for fear of losing the sunbeam. He glanced out the window at a puffy cloud lazily floating in front of the sun. He cursed under his breath, but waited for the cloud to pass.

Several minutes later, his patience paid off as the kindling began to smoke. He gently blew on the pile until a wood shaving glowed red. He blew again, turning the ember into a small flame that spread to the other shavings. He coaxed the little fire to life and now the cloth strips lit up. The flames no longer needed his help. He pushed the pile of burning strips against the wall and flames licked up the surface. Ehrich fanned the fire, feeding the flames until the wall darkened. Smoke wafted up.

Mr. Serenity would surely notice the smell, Ehrich thought. Flames now scaled the wall like a swarm of ants.

"Fire!" Ehrich yelled. "Help!"

Mr. Serenity was the first to respond, running to the cell door. As soon as he saw the growing blaze, he fumbled with his key ring until he found the key he needed. When he tried to open the cell door, however, the key wouldn't turn.

The lock was still jammed with Ehrich's hook pick. Oops.

Ehrich grabbed the cell bars and shook them. "Get me out of here!"

Mr. Serenity turned the key the other way. Nothing. The flames grew higher.

"Water!" he shouted down the hall. "Fetch water!"

"No, open the door!" Ehrich called after him.

Mr. Serenity had left the key in the lock. Ehrich grabbed the key, trying to dislodge it. The wood cracked as the fire grew larger. The key refused to budge.

The first of the water buckets arrived and the caterpillar-bearded lady swung hard, throwing water through the cell bars and against the wall. *Hiss*. Another bucket. More hissing. The flames climbed. There was no way they would douse this conflagration in time. The freaks formed a line down the hallway, passing buckets to the bearded lady. Water splashed through the bars, dousing Ehrich more than the flames. He gritted his teeth and yanked hard on the key until it popped out. The lock pick dinged against the floor. He scooped the hook pick up, then inserted the key and turned it. The lock sprang open, and he pushed the cell door. The octopus man shoved him aside and stormed into the cell. His belly expanded and he leaned forward, vomiting a powerful spray of water. The fire hissed out.

In the confusion, Ehrich slipped away from Mr. Serenity's troop, ran down the stairs and found an exit at the back of the building. As he ran down the street, Ehrich realized he had been going about the search the wrong way. If he was going to find Amina and get the answers about Dash's medallion, he would have to lure her out. What he needed was the right bait.

A LITTLE MISDIRECTION

The steam-powered boat chugged across the East River, bringing Ehrich to Devil's Island. A lanky dock guard recognized him.

"What are you doing on *our* island? Shouldn't you be doing an experiment with the mad scientist?"

Ehrich pretended to laugh. "I guess you heard."

"Commander Farrier was fuming when he crossed the bridge. What did you do to get under his skin?"

"Nothing unless you count breathing."

"You must have done something."

"I disagreed with him in front of the other hunters," Ehrich said.

"Yeah, I could see that making him fly off the handle."

"I'm sure he'll calm down," Ehrich said. He started to walk down the path.

"Hold on there, Houdini," the guard said. Apparently, Ehrich's nickname had also made the rounds. “The commander said no one gets off or on this island without his say-so.”

“Come on. I need to get my belongings. The commander didn’t even give me a chance to get my gear. I won’t be long.”

“I don’t know about this.”

“Tell you what. You let me get my things, and maybe I can sneak something from the labs for you. Tesla’s been working on some prototype weapons. He’s got a volt pistol that doesn’t use electro-darts.”

“Really?”

“You can have it, but only if you let me get my gear.”

The guard nodded. “An hour. Tops. If you see Farrier, you skedaddle.”

Ehrich thanked the guard and headed to the staff quarters. If the news had spread, there was no way he would be able to get to Ninth Circle. Not without some help. Ehrich crept to the windows of the staff dormitories and peeked inside. Wilhelm and Gino were wrestling on the floor, while Margaret and Charlie cheered them on.

Ehrich waved to catch Charlie’s attention. His friend didn’t notice him. Margaret glanced at the window and Ehrich managed to duck just in time. He waited a few minutes then peeked up again. Margaret had sandwiched herself between the two combatants to break up the fight. Gino nursed a bloody nose while Wilhelm pranced away. The German teen always took things too far.

Ehrich waved once more at Charlie. This time, he noticed. He nodded toward the far end of the building. Ehrich crouched along the bushes and made his way to the isolated area. A few minutes later, Charlie stepped out to meet him.

"Charlie, why isn't your squad on the hunt for the fugitive?"

"You're sneaking around the island so you can ask me that?"

Ehrich smiled. At least his friend still had his sense of humour.

"Farrier thinks I don't have control over my team," Charlie said with a sigh, "so he wants us to learn a hard lesson and stood us down. I don't know what you did, but he's madder than a wet hen."

"I told him he let a Dimensional escape from Demon Gate."

"Land sakes—that's why everyone's on the bug hunt! You're in hot water and the lid is coming down. Don't suppose you have a magic trick to get out of this mess."

"Actually, I might have an idea, but I need your help."

"Really? The head of Tesla's security force needs my help," Charlie joked.

Ehrich nodded. "Yes. If we bring back the fugitive, I'm pretty sure that Farrier will have to reinstate the squad."

"Farrier has the hunters scouring the city. They'll capture her before nightfall."

"I don't think so. Amina—the fugitive—is working with her sponsor, Mr. Serenity, to find someone."

"Who does she want?"

"Another Dimensional. Amazon type. Red skin. Ivory tusks out either side of her nose and a long black ponytail. I don't know who she is, but a prisoner in Ninth Circle might be connected to her." Ehrich explained.

"How do you know?"

"They both wore the same jade tael. If we can get our hands on the prisoner's tael, we might be able to fool Mr. Serenity into thinking we have the red-skinned girl. And that might be all the leverage we need to flush Amina out."

"You're baiting a trap? Not a bad idea, but if Farrier catches you traipsing around Devil's Island, he'll throw *you* in a cell."

"I'm willing to take that chance. Can you help me down to Ninth Circle?"

"Sure, I'll sneak you in under my jacket."

"We're going to need something a little better," Ehrich replied. "Like I said: you catch the fugitive, you'll be a hero. Farrier won't have any choice but to put you back in the field."

"I'm all ears. How am I going to sneak you past the guards?"

"I have an idea." Ehrich smiled.

Brian surveyed his domain, the cavern entrance to Ninth Circle. Deep beneath the surface, he ruled this fiefdom with a combination of fear and cajoling. His guards knew who was in charge and the prisoners were made to eventually understand that he controlled when they ate, when they slept, and when they had recreation. The lift lowered to the cavern, meaning that another arrival was making his or her way into his kingdom. Brian relished the thought of breaking in the new prisoner.

He watched as the lift thudded to a stop. Charlie Campbell, one of the squad leaders, had a hooded illegal in tow. Brian knew the leader from the countless times that he'd escorted illegals to Ninth Circle. Of all the hunters, Charlie apprehended the most. Brian admired his work.

"Long time no see, Charlie," the redhead joked.

"No peace for the wicked."

"Who do you have there?" Brian pointed at the hooded figure with his arms cuffed behind his back.

"Caught this illegal up north. They're calling him The Basilisk.

One look into his eyes and you're paralyzed."

"Really? How did you catch him?"

"Wasn't easy. Good thing he didn't have eyes in the back of his head. Best thing to do is keep this hood on until we get him into a cell. Then I suggest, when you feed the guy, keep your eyes to the floor."

"Thanks for the warning. I'll take you to the cells."

Charlie shook his head. "He's a slippery one. Don't want to take any more risks than I have to."

"I'll be okay," Brian insisted. He didn't like anyone questioning his ability to do his job. Even Charlie.

"Appreciate the offer, but this guy stunned two of my squad members. You don't know how to handle this kind of illegal."

"Trust me, Charlie. I've seen my share."

"Brian, just give me the keys and tell me where an isolated cell is. Someplace where he can't get a look at anyone."

The redhead puffed his chest. "This is my facility, Charlie. I handle all the prisoner entries."

"Listen, Brian. I don't mean to step on your toes here, but I want a little *alone time* with the prisoner. A little payback for what he did to my hunters."

Brian cracked a smile. "You want me to look the other way."

"If anyone asks what happened to this illegal, he did it to himself while he was in the cell."

The redhead nodded and reached for the keys around his belt. "Cell 535 should do the trick. No one's down that corridor right now. You'll have all the privacy you need."

"Thanks." Charlie took the key and climbed on the giant risers of the funicular's platform with his prisoner in tow. They sat on the angled steps.

When the platform rolled into the tunnel and they were out of sight, Charlie pulled the hood off Ehrich's head and unshackled the cuffs around his wrists.

"I sure hope you know what you're doing. You have any idea how you're going to get out?"

"Misdirection is the secret to all good magic tricks. You won't see me leaving if I make you look at something else." He picked up the keys. "Or in this case, someone else."

"You can't be serious. You're going to spring a prisoner?"

Ehrich nodded.

"Wilhelm was right. Houdini is a good nickname for you. How are you going to do it?"

"One step at a time. First, let's find Ba Tian."

When the funicular reached the bottom of the steep tunnel, the teens jumped down. Ehrich led the way through the corridors, trying to remember the route that had led him to the red-skinned Dimensional. He stopped in front of an empty cell.

"I'm sure he was right here." He paced the corridor and searched the other cells. There was no sign of Ba Tian.

"Charlie, he was in this cell. I swear."

"Then where did he go?"

"I don't know."

They expanded their search to cells in nearby corridors. "You can't miss him, Charlie. He's as big as an ox, and he's as red as roses in bloom. He's got boar tusks on the sides of his nose."

They walked past Ole Lukoje's cell. The raggedy man chuckled. "Have you come down to play with us-s-s again, fles-s-sh bag?"

"Not interested in you this time."

"Too bad. Now that you've found a new friend to play with,

he does-s-sn't s-s-seem to be around."

Ehrich stopped. "Ba Tian. You've seen him?"

"I don't know who you're talking about."

"The red-skinned prisoner down the next corridor."

Ole Lukoje leaned against his bars and smiled. "You put s-s-so many of us-s-s down here, it's-s-s hard to remember everyone."

"What do you know?" Charlie asked.

"I'm not in the busssiness-s-s of telling fles-s-sh bags-s-s anything."

Charlie stepped in. "Where's the demon? Tell us. We can make it worth your while."

The creature's shrill nasal breathing filled the cavern. "You can't give me what I want, foolis-s-sh boy."

"You want out of here. I can make that happen." Charlie bluffed.

"My friend has clout upstairs," Ehrich said, backing him up. "But if you don't cooperate, he can make your stay less than pleasant."

"Don't listen to Ehrich," Charlie said. "I only threw one prisoner in solitary and forgot about him. The rest came back to their cells after a month."

"The prisoner was so hungry he chewed off three of his fingers," Ehrich said.

"He exaggerates. It was only two." Charlie shrugged.

Ehrich glanced at Ole Lukoje for any reaction to their baiting. Nothing.

"Okay, demon, tell me what you want, I'll get it for you," Charlie said.

The raggedy man smiled. "My arm back."

The teens looked at each other, surprised.

"I didn't think s-s-so."

"Forget this one," Charlie said. "Someone else here knows where the demon went. We'll find a talker."

Ole Lukoje chuckled. "Good luck, fles-s-sh bag."

Ehrich's partner jogged down the corridor.

"He'd have better luck talking to your friends-s-s above," the raggedy man said. "They have peepers-s-s everywhere. Tas-s-sty peepers-s-s."

Ehrich turned to stare at the prisoner. For a demon to leave the prison, he'd need help, and the guards were the only ones who could give it.

"Did they let him go?"

The creature nodded. "When you know why he left, well then, that is-s-s the s-s-shocker."

"Tell me!" Ehrich ordered.

"If I tell you, the truth will haunt your nightmares-s-s for the res-s-st of your life."

"Stop wasting my time. Either you know or you don't."

Ole Lukoje crooked a finger, beckoning Ehrich to come closer. "Keep this-s-s between us-s-s. Promis-s-se?"

"Yes." Ehrich advanced to the cell door.

"What you need to know i-s-s-s that..." Ole Lukoje's sibilant voice was barely audible in the cell.

Ehrich leaned forward. Ole Lukoje's hand shot through the cage doors and clutched Ehrich's throat.

Damned misdirection, Ehrich cursed.

NINTH CIRCLE CORRUPTED

Ole Lukoje had envisioned this moment ever since he lost his arm. Now the foul creature who had dismembered him and thrown him in this filthy prison was in his grasp. The boy pushed his foot through the bars and kicked at his shins, but Ole Lukoje ignored the pain. He had his prize and he meant to claim it. He squeezed the tender flesh, wishing he had his metal talons with him now.

Charlie yanked Ehrich away from the cell, leaving Ole Lukoje clutching nothing but air. The pair fell to the floor and scrambled away from the cell.

The blond squad leader grinned. "Came back in the nick of time."

"I owe you one."

"You owe me two," Charlie reminded him.

"S-s-slippery little devil. I'll get you yet," the raggedy man said.

"Not today."

"Only a matter of time. And I'll enjoy every s-s-second of it."

Ehrich scrambled to his feet and sprinted to the funicular. He yanked the call cord as Charlie climbed on the platform.

"Did he tell you anything?"

Ehrich nodded.

"Care to share?"

"I know how the prisoner got out."

"How?" Charlie asked.

He refused to elaborate as the funicular crawled up the steep slope. Once the cable car rolled out of the tunnel, Ehrich hopped off and sprinted to the guardhouse. Brian stepped out, surprised to see the dark-haired teen. Ehrich grabbed a fistful of Brian's red hair as he hauled him across the uneven cavern floor and wrestled him into a headlock on his knees. Charlie followed the pair as a half dozen guards poured out of the guardhouse.

"Let go!" Brian squealed.

"What did you do?" Ehrich demanded.

"Ow!"

"The prisoner. The big one with red skin. He's not there anymore. What did you do?"

The guards drew their weapons. Charlie motioned them to stand down. They eyed their leader, then Charlie, unsure of what to do.

Ehrich whirled on the others with Brian still in his grasp. "What did you do with the prisoner?"

The teens lowered their weapons, their glances darting uncertainly at one another.

Brian wheezed, "No idea... what you're talking... about. All the prisoners are... accounted for."

"The one with the tusks. And the jade tael necklace. He's as big as a bear."

"You were... seeing things," Brian choked out.

"Tell me where you put him." Ehrich slammed the teen's head into the ground. "Tell me!"

Charlie pulled his friend back. "Easy, Ehrich. You're losing it."

"I need to talk to the prisoner. Now!"

"Look, if they didn't see him, they didn't see him. You can't squeeze water out of ashes. Let's go."

"What? They know what's going on."

Charlie hauled Ehrich off of Brian and shoved him across the cavern out of earshot. He whispered, "You're like a damn dog with a bone. Back off for a second. They've obviously made some deal with this demon. You said there's a breach in security. Well, we found it. Now we can take it to Farrier."

Charlie was right. Though Ehrich didn't like the commander, he knew the man would never allow corruption on his island. He alone had the authority to compel Brian to confess. Before a groggy Brian or his guards could react, the two boys climbed into the lift and pulled the lever to ascend to the surface.

Ehrich paced the mesh cage, seething.

"Why would they let this prisoner go?" Charlie asked.

"Ba Tian claimed he was a merchant. He offered me whatever I wanted. I bet Brian and his pals had a price."

"Nothing's worth risking your job," Charlie said.

"Unless it's valuable enough that you would never have to work again," Ehrich said.

His friend nodded. When the lift reached the surface, Ehrich and Charlie sought George Farrier in his office. The reception area was empty and so was the commander's office.

"Bet he went to the mess hall for dinner. Let's go, Ehrich."

"No. Let's wait here. I don't want anyone else eavesdropping in case they're in on it."

"Good point." Charlie plopped into a chair.

Ehrich paced, his body as wired with energy as his mind. How was the red giant connected to the red-skinned girl? Was it coincidence that they wore the same jade tael? Or was he an ally working with the girl? When Mr. Serenity talked about the asset, was he talking about the red-skinned giant? What did the behemoth offer the guards to buy his freedom? Most troubling of all: what was Ba Tian going to do now that he was free?

On a shelf, Ehrich noticed a glint as the sun's rays shone through the large bay window. He leaned closer to examine the item. A jade tael with a square hole in the coin's centre—exactly like the jade tael necklace the crimson-skinned behemoth and the red-skinned girl wore around their necks. Ehrich's blood went cold as he recalled the girl's message: *This jade tael belongs to the House of Qi. Let the tael be a symbol of our alliance.*

"Charlie, how does Farrier get all these things?"

"He collects them from the demons. Why?"

Ehrich picked up the tael. "Because I saw a tael like this on Ba Tian."

"What are you saying?"

"I think Farrier had a hand in letting the prisoner go."

"What? No. Not possible."

"Charlie, maybe Amina could have slipped past a sleepy guard in the Dimensional dormitories and jumped out a window, but Ba Tian was in Ninth Circle. You think he can just stroll out of the tunnel and climb on the lift without someone spotting him?"

"Guess not."

"Someone higher up would have to make sure people weren't going to sound the alarm. And Ba Tian said this tael was worth more than anything we had in this dimension. It's supposed to be a symbol of alliance."

"Why would the commander let a demon go?" Charlie asked.

Before Ehrich could answer, footsteps echoed outside the door. Farrier was back.

FLEEING DEVIL'S ISLAND

Commander George Farrier's day couldn't end fast enough. The business with Amina the fugitive had everyone scrambling around the island and into New York. If word of this escape leaked out, he would have to answer to the mayor and he didn't need any attention drawn to his operations.

Behind him, a mousy clerk with blond hair and spectacles hounded him. "Sir, how should I report the incident to the mayor's office?"

"Tarnation! You don't."

"But sir, the people need to be warned."

"There is one thing I need immediately and that is for you to be silent."

"Excuse me, sir?"

"No. No. That's not silence. Once more, I'm sure you will succeed this time."

"Commander?"

"Disappointing. Not to worry, you'll have plenty of time to practise on burial detail. I'd say three weeks should do. Off you toddle."

The stunned girl turned and scurried away, only now having learned to keep quiet. Farrier shook his head. Soldiers took orders. Bureaucrats took his patience. He hobbled to the door and grabbed the handle.

Inside Farrier's office, Ehrich searched for a hiding place, but there was none. Charlie headed for the desk. Ehrich waved him back as the door handle turned. He rushed to the door and yanked it open, pulling an off-balance Farrier into the room. Ehrich shoved the man to the floor and Charlie leapt over him. Then they both bolted through the doorway and down the hallway before the dazed commander could find his bearings or identify the intruders.

The boys sprinted toward the dock where Ehrich's boat was waiting.

"Farrier can't be in on this," Charlie panted as they rounded the corner approaching the pier. "We need to go back."

"I can't take the chance. If he's part of the corruption, what do you think he'll do to us?"

"Back so soon?" the lanky sentinel from the guardhouse called out to them. Then he noticed the commotion spilling out of the building. "What happened in there? Another escape?" The sentinel cocked his head to the side. "What did you do, Houdini?"

Without losing any speed, the muscular Weisz slammed his fist into the boy's midsection and kneed him in the chin, knocking him out.

"Did you really need to do that?" Charlie asked.

"Didn't know what else to do."

"Next time, try a magic trick, Houdini."

Ehrich ignored the jab and climbed into the boat. "There's got to be someone we can tell about this. Maybe the mayor? The newspapers?"

"We have no evidence."

"Help me find proof." He motioned Charlie to join him in the boat.

Charlie shook his head. "I'm already in enough trouble as it is."

"If Farrier finds out you were helping me, he's not just going to demote you. He's going to kick you off the squad. That's harder for him to do if you have Amina in your custody."

"You sure you know where to find her?"

"No, but it's a better shot than waiting for them." Ehrich pointed to several guards now making their way toward the dock. "Make up your mind fast."

"Man alive, you're nothing but trouble sometimes."

"You coming?"

Charlie took one last look behind him then joined his friend. They pushed off from the shore and Ehrich fired up the steam engine as they motored away from the island.

"Want to tell me where we're headed?" Charlie said.

"We're going to pay the Museum of Curiosities a visit."

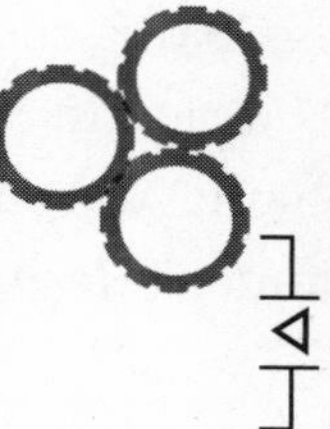

STAKE OUT

Manhattan's shoreline drew closer as the launch bounced across the waves of the East River. Ehrich revved the steam engine to full speed and the paddle wheel turned faster. The breeze felt good against his face. Ahead, the ships moored at the ports grew closer. Their skeleton masts were bare of sails, but they were still impressive. Beyond the shipyard, the buildings of New York rose up to the cloudy sky.

He recalled standing on the deck of the *Frisia*, the ship that had brought him to America. His America. He and Dash marvelled at the New York skyline as the liner sailed into harbour. His young brother grabbed his hand and pointed at the giant spire of the Trinity Church, the tallest structure on Manhattan at the time. This was before the Brooklyn Bridge, before the Statue of Liberty—before dimension portals.

The sea spray hit his face, pulling him from his reverie. Charlie hunched over the bow and retched. He'd never make a good sailor. Once they reached Manhattan, Ehrich knew he'd have to move quickly. It would only be a matter of time before the guard came to and Farrier sent hunters after them. He hoped Charlie's seasickness wouldn't slow them too much. He piloted the launch toward the nearest open berth and tied off the boat while Charlie climbed on to the dock.

"You okay to run?"

Charlie waved him off. "Feeling better already. Hold on a minute." He puked again and wiped his mouth. "Now I'm ready."

"Let's go."

Rather than run all the way down to the Bowery, Ehrich headed to the elevated train station. The ride cost them a nickel each, but they would put some distance between them and the hunters. They were in luck. When they arrived at the platform, a train was about to pull out. Billowing smoke from the engine's stack choked the air. The boys jumped through the open doors and found a seat near a pair of uptown ladies.

The women dusted dirt from their patterned paletots and eyed Ehrich's grimy duster and Charlie's soiled trousers. Charlie tugged his bowler over his eyes and gazed out the window. The ladies shifted in their seats, creating a separation between them and the unkempt sweaty young men.

As the train clacked along the elevated rail, Ehrich surveyed the sooty buildings along the line. People teemed on the streets. A sour-faced woman hung clothes on a line outside her third-story window. He thought of his mother hanging clothes and wondered what she would be doing now. He longed to see her, but he knew he couldn't go back. Not yet.

Charlie leaned over. "I've been thinking. Farrier's taking a big chance letting the prisoner go."

"Everyone has a price."

"Maybe." The blond boy fell silent for a moment, then: "You saw what Ole Lukoje did. How could Farrier be sure this Ba Tian wasn't as dangerous? What did the demon pay to get out?"

Charlie's question sat uneasily on Ehrich's mind as the train pulled into the next station. The haughty women stepped off, casting one final glance at the dirty boys. Ehrich tipped his bowler and flashed them a devil-may-care grin. The older woman frowned, but the younger woman smiled at Ehrich's showman gesture.

The next stop was theirs. Ehrich hopped off the train with Charlie close behind. The boys climbed down the platform stairs and navigated the crowds of vendors and onlookers until they reached their destination. A closed sign hung in the window beside the door. Odd to have an establishment closed in the afternoon. Ehrich suspected Mr. Serenity was waiting for Amina to show up and wanted no other unwelcome visitors.

"Now what?" Charlie asked.

"We wait for Amina."

"Man alive, that's your plan? How do you know she'll even come here?"

"The Demon Gate clerk. Remember cotton nose?"

Charlie nodded.

"He asked her who her sponsor was. She mentioned the Museum."

"Don't you think the other hunters are going to make it down here, then?"

Ehrich shook his head. "By the time someone figures out to

talk to the processing clerk, we'll have nabbed her."

His friend watched the pedestrians moving along the street. "As long as the hunters don't collar us first. The Bowery is probably the first place they'll look once they figure out we were the ones snooping around Farrier's office."

"Why would you think that?"

"Because it's where they'd go if they were on the run. You always go back to your roots," Charlie said, referring to the fact that every member of Demon Watch had once been an orphan who spent time on the Bowery's streets. "When all else fails, go back to what's familiar—and for all of us, this place was home."

Ehrich nodded. "We'd better find her fast. Maybe someone saw something. We should canvas the shop owners."

Charlie agreed and they split up to ask around. Ehrich popped into the lunch shop across the street. The cramped quarters offered little room for the impatient patrons waiting for meat pies. Tattered red drapes adorned the dining area walls, barely hiding a cockroach skittering up the wall. Ehrich pushed past the diners.

"Out of the way."

"Brat," a gruff man spat out.

"Wait your turn," a common woman in a dusty checkered dress yelled.

"I'll be fast." Ehrich then asked the owner, "I need some information."

The balding man wiped his hands on his dirty apron. "You want pies, I got 'em. You want to talk, go to the rum hole next door."

"This is official Demon Watch business."

"Bully for you, kid. I have a real business with real hungry customers."

The impatient crowd grumbled. The woman in the checkered dress left the shop.

"I've got time to stand here all day, mister," Ehrich said. "Not sure if your customers do. Now are you going to give me some answers?"

Another customer left.

"Fine, fine," the owner said. "What do you want to know? Quick."

"Has anyone been in or out of the Museum of Curiosities today?"

"How should I know? I'm up to my ears in orders."

"Know why they're closed now?"

"Who cares? They're demons and freaks over there. They can close permanently for all I care. You got any other questions?"

"No," Ehrich said. He shoved through the crowd and received a few anonymous elbow jabs along the way.

Every shop owner had the same answer. Even the street vendors took no notice of the comings and goings of the Museum. When Charlie returned, he had the same news to report. No one had seen anything.

Charlie sighed. "Well, it looks like we're in for a long day. You know what would make the time go by faster? Some grub."

Ehrich agreed.

They walked over to an oyster vendor who tried to entice them to buy his smelly wares. "Here's oysters, here's oysters. All the way from Rockaway. They're good to eat. They're good to fry. They're good for an oyster pot pie."

"You got money, Ehrich? I'm starving."

He fished out the few coins he had in his pocket and paid for his friend's meal. They lingered on the street, sucking the juicy morsels out of the shell. The slimy oyster slid down Ehrich's throat and silenced the grumbling in his stomach. Through the rest of the afternoon, people passed by. Some slowed to haggle with vendors, but New Yorkers were a busy lot, and none lingered for long. Ehrich leaned against the iron pillar of the elevated railroad and kept an eye out for hunters. None had shown up yet. Most likely, they'd start north and work their way downtown.

Charlie nudged him and nodded at the corner, where a newsie was hawking papers.

"Extra, extra. Get your *World* here. Two cents," the hawk-nosed boy in a cap and tattered jacket yelled as he waved a paper around in his hands. He anchored his foot on a stack of papers to keep them from flying away or being stolen.

"Am I glad those days are behind us," Charlie said.

"I didn't mind. It was fun to see how much I could make in a day."

"You got corn for brains? All the nights we had to sleep under the papers we didn't sell? No, thank you."

"Charlie, you remember the day your papers blew away? I've never seen you scramble like that. You looked like a crab."

"How could I forget? Split my pants. Banged my knee. Couple of newsies thought I was horning in on their turf. They gave me a damn good shiner."

"Hey, I got there before they really roughed you up."

"Learned to stand on my papers after that. This newsie probably picked up the trick from me."

Ehrich laughed. "Yeah, they're probably telling each other, 'Don't pull a Charlie Campbell.'"

"You're hurting my feelings, Ehrich."

"Aw. Sorry."

"Feed me and I'll think about forgiving you."

Ehrich cracked a grin and gave his friend the last of his money so he could order another oyster. As Charlie bickered with the vendor for the largest oyster, Ehrich glanced around. He had the distinct feeling someone was watching him. He looked up at the track overhead. He scanned the street. A trio of guttersnipes ducked away from an angry shop owner. Peddlers tried to snare the attention of passers-by. A woman shooed away a dog. Nothing suspicious. Ehrich shook off the feeling and found a place to watch the Museum.

Ehrich and Charlie took turns staking out the place. Charlie had found a stoop to sleep on when he wasn't on duty. Through the night, Ehrich watched the Museum entrance, but no one showed up, and no one left. He started to feel his eyelids grow heavy as the arc lamps sparked to life. He nudged Charlie awake.

"Your turn," Ehrich said.

Charlie let out a yawn. "Nothing to report?"

"No movement."

His friend stretched and stood up. "I sure hope this leads to something because I don't think I've got a job to go back to."

Ehrich shook his head. "Our squad's scored the highest capture rate. There's no way Farrier is going to lose one of his best squad leaders."

"Yeah, but I can't seem to keep my hunters in check."

"Now you can. I'm no longer on your squad."

"Oh, right. You found yourself a little promotion." He smiled.

"Yes. I'm the caretaker of guinea pigs."

"Don't get too big for your britches," Charlie warned. "Happened to me the first time I became squad leader. I was in love with the idea of being in charge. Then I realized that I could lose it all if I didn't have the hunters' respect."

"You had our respect?" Ehrich joked. "That's news to me."

Charlie chuckled.

"You ever think what you'd do if you didn't have the squad, Charlie?"

"This is the only life I know. I couldn't go back on the streets. And getting a regular job, well, who's going to hire me? I've got no skills other than shooting demons. Besides, without the high stakes of a bug hunt, I'd go mad. What about you? What would you do?"

"I'd like to try my hand at show business."

"Oh, right. Houdini."

Ehrich smiled. "That name's kind of growing on me."

"Ehrich Houdini?"

"No. That would look terrible on a poster. No one would know how to pronounce my first name. I'd need something flashier."

"The Mysterious Houdini," Charlie offered.

"Maybe some alliteration," Ehrich suggested.

"Horace Houdini."

"No."

"Howard Houdini."

"Ugh." Ehrich turned his nose at the name.

"Henry?"

"The king of magicians. Not bad."

"Harry Houdini?"

"I like the sound of that."

Charlie sat up. "So, Harry Houdini, show me a trick."

"I wasn't planning on entertaining anyone. I left everything back at the dormitory."

Charlie chuckled. "I'm sure Wilhelm is rifling through it now to see what else he can break."

"Okay, I've got a simple trick. Watch this." Ehrich grabbed his right thumb with his left hand and grunted as he pulled. His right thumb separated from the knuckle. Then he reassembled the thumb.

Charlie's eyes were big and wide as he leaned forward. "That is so amazing. I can't believe you actually think you have a career in magic with that lame trick. Come on, now. Why are you even interested in magic anyway?"

Ehrich stretched out on the stoop and yawned. "I don't know. When I was a kid, my dad used to take me to those travelling entertainment shows. Nothing spectacular, but one of the acts featured a magician. He did card tricks. He made a coin disappear. Then he made a rabbit disappear in a box. Everyone in the audience was amazed. They had no idea how he did the tricks and they were buzzing for the rest of the show. I begged my father to take me backstage so that I could ask the magician how he made the rabbit disappear. So he did. When I asked the magician how he made the rabbit disappear, he refused to tell me. I begged him to tell me, but he said the secret to being a good magician was to let the audience see what he wants them to see and not what they want to see." Ehrich paused, thinking how much the magician's comment reminded him of Tesla's advice about selling his inventions.

"So you never found out how the rabbit trick worked?" Charlie asked.

"I didn't say that. My father and the magician started talking about something else and, while they were looking the other way, I peeked in the box."

"How does the rabbit trick work?"

Ehrich put his fingers to his lips and shushed his friend with a knowing smile.

"You have to tell me," Charlie begged.

The dark-haired teen shook his head. "I loved how the mystery of the disappearing rabbit made me want to learn more. After my father and I left, I overheard people raving about the magician. Right then, I decided I wanted to have that kind of life."

"I wish I'd known my father. What happened to yours? How did he die?"

Ehrich wanted to tell his friend that his father was still alive but in another dimension. Most likely, he would be preparing a sermon as his primary duty as the rabbi in Appleton, Wisconsin. But for him to tell the truth would mean to expose himself as the very illegal Dimensional that Charlie and he had sworn to apprehend. Instead, he borrowed Tesla's story. "He fell off his horse."

"I'm sorry, Ehrich. At least you had a chance to be with your father. My mother, before she died, said that mine was a drifter and no good to the family. She said we were better off without him. I don't know if she was right or not, but that doesn't matter now. We're all in the same boat."

Ehrich smiled. "Well, after I saw how you threw up, I don't think I want you in my boat again."

Charlie punched his friend in the arm. "Shut up. You know I can't stand small boats."

Ehrich rubbed his arm. "Okay, I'm going to get some sleep. Wake me if you see anyone."

He curled into a ball and drifted off to sleep.

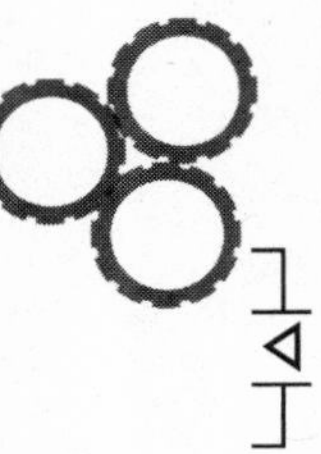

THE JADE TAEL

In the heart of the Bowery, men clashed with one another in a bloody gang war. Ehrich stood up from the cobblestone road and scanned the melee. Dash stood in the middle. He reached out for Ehrich. Then a bloom of blood appeared on his shirt. The boy crumpled like a limp doll. Ehrich rushed to help him, but the battle surged in between the two and he found himself being pushed back farther and farther. He couldn't save his brother. The boy stared at Ehrich and gasped, "Help me!"

"Dash!" Ehrich bolted up, drenched in sweat. His brother haunted his nightmares and the sting of his failure still made his heart ache. Above the Bowery, the sky was starting to lighten.

Charlie snored beside him.

"You were supposed to keep watch," Ehrich said. He kicked his friend, who awoke with a start.

"I was resting my eyes," Charlie protested. "My ears were

wide open."

Ehrich climbed to his feet and stretched. Vendors and shop owners made their way along the street as life returned to the Bowery. As Ehrich stepped on the sidewalk, he noticed a couple approaching the Museum. The gentleman wore a smart black waistcoat while his female companion wore a yellow foulard bodice and bustle. A veil covered her face and white gloves covered her hands. The pair stopped outside the Museum, glancing around the street. Then they started up the steps. He wished he could see under the veil. Perhaps this was Amina. If so, who was her male companion?

He ran across the street, stumbling toward the pair. Charlie fell in step beside his partner. The woman glanced back and tugged her companion's arm. They moved away from the Museum. Ehrich moved closer on an intercept course. When he was within arm's reach, he noticed the woman had a necklace. On the end of the strap was a jade tael—a round coin with a square hole in the centre. The symbol of the House of Qi.

"Excuse me," he said, bumping into the woman.

She didn't respond. Instead, the couple sped away, heading north under the Sixth Avenue elevated train. Ehrich waved at Charlie.

"Is it Amina?" Charlie asked.

"No, but I think it's the one Amina is looking for. We have to go after them."

"What about the Museum?"

"You watch the door." He sprinted after the pair.

"Oh no, you're not freelancing on me," Charlie said grimly. "Wait up!"

Ehrich matched the couple's pace but stayed far enough back so as not to be noticed. The gentleman stopped at a peddler and browsed the assortment of dried goods on the cart while the woman scanned the street. Charlie caught up to Ehrich, but a guttersnipe grabbed the back of his duster.

"Spare some change?" the child begged.

"Let go," Charlie said.

The woman grabbed the man's arm, and the pair dashed away. Ehrich gave chase but Charlie couldn't shake free of the urchin. The couple rounded a corner and Ehrich followed.

Suddenly, a red hand grabbed him by the throat and slammed him against the brick wall.

"Why are you following us?" the woman hissed through her veil. Close up, Ehrich noticed tiny ivory tusks protruding from either side of her flared nostrils. "Who are you?"

"Nobody," he gasped.

Her grip tightened as she lifted him off his feet.

"What do you want with us?" she asked.

Her friend grabbed her arm and glanced over his shoulder. "We're in the open, Ning Shu. We should go."

She nodded, beginning to squeeze her grip firmer. Ehrich gasped for air.

"No. Not that way."

The red-skinned girl continued to choke the life out of Ehrich.

Charlie raced around the corner. "Hey! Drop him!"

The gentleman raised his arm and a spring-loaded derringer shot out of his sleeve and into his hand. The tiny pistol had a series of spinning gears along the barrel which instantly telescoped to triple its original length.

"Gun!" Ehrich gasped.

A whistle pierced the air and a dart flew into the man's neck. He clutched at it and staggered back.

The red-skinned woman tossed Ehrich to the ground and whirled around, yanking off her jade tael necklace. She whipped it around in the air, creating a vortex that solidified into a glowing blue force field. A second dart bounced off the shield and landed on the sidewalk.

"Hakeem, are you all right?" she cried out to her companion.

He plucked the dart from his neck and clutched the tiny weapon. "Yes."

"We must go," she shouted. She angled the spinning jade tael toward the brick wall of the nearby building. A part of the wall exploded and bricks fell to the granite, forcing Ehrich to roll out of the way. Dust rose from the falling debris. Ehrich coughed as he climbed to his feet. He ran into Charlie.

"Did you see who shot?" he asked his friend.

Charlie pointed to a rooftop. "No, but it came from up there."

Ehrich nodded. "Try to track the shooter. I'll go after the other two."

"Sure. Watch yourself. Meet back at the Museum."

"Got it." He ran after the couple.

Charlie turned his gaze skyward, catching the glimpse of a small figure running from one rooftop to another. The shooter moved fast, reaching the last building on the block before disappearing from the rooftop's edge. Charlie ran to the brick building and kept his eye on the street level door. A dark-haired boy emerged a few moments later, tucking a crossbow under his jacket as he strode down the busy street.

Charlie fell in step behind the shooter all the way through Greenwich. The brownstone apartments soon gave way to warehouse buildings, and Charlie picked up the pace, realizing the boy was going to run out of real estate before he reached the Hudson River.

At the end of Morton Street, past a horse stable, the shooter jogged toward an excavation site. Two muscular men tended the entrance, but they seemed to recognize the boy and granted him entry.

Charlie stepped closer and noticed a sign on the fence: "Haskins' Hudson River Tunnel Project." Counting the many demons making their way through the gate, Ehrich guessed this project must be pretty massive. Why would workers in a river tunnel project need these two demons dead? He pulled his collar up and leaned against the brick wall. And waited.

Far away from the Hudson River, Ehrich struggled to keep up with the Dimensionals. They navigated the streets, always moving north, then headed up the stairs leading to the Ninth Avenue elevated train platform.

Ehrich reached the steps as a gaggle of commuters was coming down. He struggled to wade through the crowd, grabbing the railing to keep from being pushed back and knocking a couple of people out of his way. But just above him, the train began to pull out of the station, heading south. He had lost them.

Or so he thought. The sound of footsteps behind him caught his attention and he turned around. The pair was hustling along the railroad tracks in the opposite direction of the departing train. Ehrich ran along the platform and hopped onto the tracks.

At that moment, another train approached from the north. He stepped over to the other track, but the couple didn't stray from their collision course with the oncoming engine.

A whistle shrilled.

Ehrich screamed, "Get off the track!"

He turned his head and squeezed his eyes shut as the whistle screamed one last time before the inevitable impact.

Once the train rolled into the station, however, Ehrich saw no trace of carnage on the track in its wake. Had the couple been knocked off the elevated rails? He surveyed the street far below. Nothing. They had vanished.

UNDER THE HUDSON RIVER

Ehrich returned to Mr. Serenity's Museum of Curiosities. He pushed through the throng of vendors and gawkers wending their way through the neighbourhood in search of entertainment at one of the local theatres or a drink at one of the taverns in the area. A spiritualist tried to hand him a pamphlet claiming that the existence of Dimensionals spelled the end of the world. She reminded him of Madame Mancini. Ehrich shoved it away.

Across the street from the Museum, Charlie flirted with a hot corn vendor. She handed him two ears of corn. He could turn on the charm when he had to.

"Any luck?" he asked Ehrich.

He shook his head and told the bizarre story of how he had lost the couple on the elevated tracks.

"What about you, Charlie?"

"You're going to love this. The shooter was a kid."

"Might be a Dimensional. Looks can be deceiving," Ehrich reminded his friend.

"Sure, sure. Whatever the demon was, he ran to the Hudson River. You know the tunnel project?"

Ehrich shook his head.

"The demons are working for some rail tycoon named Haskins. They're building a tunnel under the river to connect trains between New Jersey and Manhattan. It's supposed to save money, but the danger of the river collapsing on the tunnel is why only demons are willing to do the job. The weird thing is that the guys they have working there are generally the size of small horses. What use would they have of a kid? I think there's something more going on here."

"You sure he's still there?"

"Yeah, should be. Found an urchin to watch the entrance anyway, so we'll know if he leaves and where he ends up. Want to check it out?"

Ehrich smiled. "Show me the way."

The pair arrived at the Hudson River Tunnel Project in time for a shift change. Labourers lined up in front of the gate, waiting to go through. As Ehrich looked at the Dimensionals, he wondered how desperate for work they had to be to risk their lives under the Hudson River.

The morning sun glared down on Ehrich as he lugged a stack of newspapers under his arm. His stomach growled and he knew he'd have to sell quite a few papers if he was going to buy today's meal. Before a nearby six-story clothing factory, a crowd gathered. Maybe he could make an easy sale or two. He jogged toward the scene, but slowed when he spotted the reason for the mob.

The angry protestors blocked the entrance to the building. Namely, they kept out the ragtag collection of workers showing up for their shift. In contrast to the grubby faces of the human protestors, the crimson-skinned labourers looked like demons from the underworld. Some towered over the others like tall oaks against saplings. A few sported tusks from their temples. A woman had black braided hair that resembled octopus tentacles. They were Dimensionals, beings from other worlds, like himself.

"Scabs!" yelled a voice in the angry mob. Ehrich couldn't see who shouted, but he guessed that the safety of the mob spurred on the rabble-rouser. Soon, other people echoed the sentiment, until it built into a chant punctuated with insults. "Demons! Go back to where you came from! You don't belong here!"

Ehrich stiffened and began to back away. He had seen this happen before at other factories and workplaces, where rich owners replaced human labour with Dimensionals willing to work for less. He wanted to tell the mob to direct their anger at the greedy factory owner rather than at the Dimensionals, who were just trying to earn enough to feed their families, but he knew it was easier for the mob to hate those who looked different and he was relieved he didn't look like the frightened labourers.

A rock flew into the group of workers and struck a tall man in overalls, drawing what appeared to be green blood from his wide forehead. The Dimensionals closed ranks. Emboldened, the mob surged ahead and another stone flew. Then another. A blue-skinned behemoth caught one of the flying projectiles and tossed it in his mouth. He chewed rapidly, then leaned forward and spewed tiny pellets at the mob. The front line of protestors fell to the ground, clutching their faces in agony. This was enough to set off the riot.

Men and women charged the Dimensionals. Sticks came out and several workers fell under the barrage of beatings, until the woman with the tentacle hair wielded her braids like whips and lashed the protestors' weapons out of their hands. The mob swarmed over the outnumbered labourers and the fighting spilled across the street in front of the factory.

Ehrich hoisted the papers under his arm and backed away from the battle. A short golden-skinned worker with bushy eyebrows and a torn smock emerged from the scene. She was barely older than ten and the right side of her face had puffed up from a protestor's attack. She reached up with a clawed hand to wipe the green blood streaming from her forehead. Her thick eyebrows reminded Ehrich of his brother Dash.

Two burly men descended on the injured Dimensional. One grabbed her arm while the other raised his hand to strike her. Ehrich rushed at the attackers and hurled his stack of newspapers high in the air. The explosion of papers distracted the men from the wounded child. Ehrich blasted through the falling blizzard of newsprint, grabbed the girl's arm and yanked her away from the crowd.

He rounded a corner and peeked back. The men kicked his papers across the ground and rejoined the fray. Ehrich's ruse had worked, but there was no way he'd recover the money he spent to buy the newspapers. He'd have to go hungry another day or find a portly street vendor he could outrun.

"You'll be fine here," he assured the frightened girl.

Her green pupils widened and her nostrils flared. She stammered, "W-w-what do you want from me?"

"Nothing."

She shrank back against the wall. "They warned me about your kind."

"Land sakes, we're not all the same. I'm not going to hurt you."

The yellow-skinned girl eyed him, unsure.

He peeked around the corner. "That riot will not be over quickly. You're safer here."

She stiffened. "My mother! She's still there. I have to help her."

Ehrich grabbed her arm. "Listen, I don't know your mother, but I do not think she would want you in harm's way."

"I told her we shouldn't go to work today," the girl muttered. "I have to go."

"You know what my mother did? We were on a ship coming to America. My father was already in New York, so she had to care for all five kids by herself. When it was time to eat, some of the other passengers, they would elbow their way to the front of the line and take more than their share. My mother, she saw this and didn't think it was fair that her kids starved so that these men could eat. So she pushed past them to get enough food for all of us. She was a tiny woman, but everyone backed down to her. I will guess your mother is much like mine, yes?"

Her hunched shoulders finally relaxed. He patted her claw hand. The clamour of battle raged on around the corner, but the space Ehrich had created for this girl was quiet and still. She took his wrist in her claw and smiled. "Yes, she is."

"She will be fine," Ehrich said. "You and I are the same."

An explosion ripped through the air, startling both of them. A sharp pain radiated around his wrist, where the girl was now squeezing her claw.

"What are you doing?" he gasped.

"Momma!" the frightened girl cried.

She bolted around the corner, leaving Ehrich clutching his bloody wrist to stem the flow of blood from his jagged wound. He scanned the crowd but the girl was gone.

Charlie approached an urchin, a dirty-faced human girl, leaning against a brick wall that gave her the perfect vantage point to spy on the comings and goings of the Hudson River Tunnel Project. She eyed the cobs of corn Charlie held in his hand and licked her lips.

"Did you see anyone leave, kid?"

"Cost you to know," she said.

He gave her one of the cobs.

She shucked the warm corn and bit into the cob. "No. No kids went out or in."

"You're sure? You didn't look away or go off someplace?"

She shook her head.

"Good job." He gave her the other cob. "Now scram."

She ran off.

Ehrich eyed the entrance. "You ready for this?"

"I'd feel a lot more ready if I had a volt pistol with me," Charlie said as he strode ahead toward the gate.

They cut to the front of the line. Ehrich tipped his bowler to the attendants. "Afternoon, gentlemen."

"What do you want?" the bald one with serpent tattoos around his neck asked.

Charlie crossed his arms over his chest. "We heard some reports that a few illegals might be working here."

"No. We run a clean operation," the other guard replied. "Isn't that right, Jinn?"

The tattooed one nodded.

Charlie didn't give up. "My partner is a stickler for details. We'd like to do a spot inspection."

"I'll say one thing for you hunters: you're thorough, as in thorough pains in the neck," Jinn said.

Ehrich slid beside his friend. The hulking attendants, likely to have more muscle than sense and more scars than teeth, refused to budge.

"Listen fellas, you know the Demon Watch is going to go into your operations sooner or later," Charlie said. "A spot check won't put a crimp in your night, but it'd be a shame if Mr. Haskins found out you could have avoided a weeklong shutdown."

"Two weeks, Charlie."

Jinn eyed Ehrich for a second, then sighed. He turned to his companion. "Mind the store. I'll be back."

He led the pair through the line-up of labourers shuffling toward a giant pit near the shoreline. Dimensionals lowered themselves down a series of ladders into a quarry. Ehrich glanced at the workers around him and imagined how easy it was to be mistaken for one of them. Granted some had different coloured skin, a few had multiple arms and one had two heads, but besides the few anomalies, many of the Dimensionals appeared as human as any New Yorker.

As they descended, Ehrich noticed a purple-skinned labourer in denim overalls with a white mohawk climbing down a ladder ahead of them. On second glance, however, Ehrich realized the mohawk was actually bone shards jutting from the man's skull.

All the others seemed to be going out of their way to give him plenty of room.

"How much farther down do we have to go?" Charlie asked their tattooed escort.

Jinn smiled. "All the way down."

When they finally reached the bottom, the workers pulled picks and shovels from open boxes at the bottom of the ladders and entered a wide tunnel. In the dim glow from lanterns, Ehrich could barely see the bone-shard mohawk of the giant labourer as he and many others walked into an airlock. A giant vault door closed, leaving Ehrich, Charlie and the other workers to wait their turn. A loud hiss filled the air followed by a tremor in the ground. The workers shuffled closer to the vault door.

Charlie nudged Ehrich and whispered, "The kid has dark hair. I think he was wearing a brown jacket and black trousers."

Ehrich scanned the crowd of massive labourers. Even Charlie seemed like a child among these titans. "So, basically, anyone who doesn't look like them."

Charlie nodded. A few workers glared at the pair, recognizing the hunter dusters. Ehrich returned their stares. "Never show a sign of weakness," was something his mother had taught him. The moment you show fear is the moment the other person has you. He wasn't about to let the workers know he was afraid.

After a few minutes, the vault door hissed opened and the workers trudged into the airlock. Ehrich and Charlie joined the crowd inside the pressurized chamber. The smooth iron walls seemed to want to close in on Ehrich. He stared at the other vault door, willing it to open. Ehrich wondered how much air this giant milk churn could hold. His thoughts wandered to Robert Houdin: If the magician had attempted escapes, how would he have escaped from here? The lock pick in the heel of Ehrich's right shoe wouldn't be enough. He would need a wrench to undo the giant bolts holding the vault door. But Ehrich was no professional escape artist, so all he could do for now was wait for the door to open.

Finally, a worker spun the wheel on the vault door and a loud pop echoed in the chamber as the door swung open. On the other side, Ehrich witnessed misery personified. Hundreds of workers toiled in the giant tunnel, attacking the rock and carrying it away in wheelbarrows. The rank odour of sweat assaulted Ehrich's nose. Arc lamps located throughout the tunnel cast some light but not enough to chase away the oppressive darkness.

The workers seemed to congregate with their own kind. Red skins with red skins; blue with blue; giant heads with other giant heads. Rarely did he see one group intermingling with another. Not a single labourer stood shorter than six feet.

Charlie and Ehrich made their way around the tunnel, pushing past the Dimensionals who were wheeling carts full of rock. A team of red-skinned titans brandished giant iron paddles and hacked at the bigger chunks of rock with lightning speed, pulverizing it into small pebbles. Another team of green-hued labourers scooped up the pebbles with hoses attached to giant packs on their backs. At the far end of the tunnel, other labourers wearing the same packs fired their hoses of pebbles at the wall, breaking off large pieces of the rock. It was a self-perpetuating process of using the rock broken down to break up more rocks. Ehrich and Charlie walked the length of the tunnel and back several times, scanning the faces of the sweaty Dimensionals. When they returned to the airlock vault door, the tattooed man glanced at them.

Jinn grunted at the pair. “Seen enough yet?”

“We’ll let you know when we’re done,” Charlie said.

“I don’t see any kids here,” Ehrich whispered. “Maybe your scout was lying when she said no one left.”

“I guess it’s possible.”

“Besides, why would a kid be down here in the first place?”

Charlie turned to the tattooed man. “Do you have kids working down here?”

Jinn flared his nostrils, indignant. “You can call us demons and monsters, but we’re not heartless like your kind. We don’t make our children work in these conditions—ever. Now, if you’re done here, I have to get back to my job.”

Charlie glanced at Ehrich and shrugged. They had lost their quarry. They motioned to Jinn and he opened the vault door. With the last of the shift workers in the tunnel, the airlock was now empty. They stepped inside as the tattooed man shut the vault door. Ehrich glanced around the smooth surface of the walls. Then he stiffened.

“Charlie, when we came down here, do you remember seeing the purple Dimensional? The one with the bone shards coming out of his skull?”

“Yeah, that demon’s going to star in my nightmares for the next ten years. Couldn’t miss him.”

“Did you see him in the tunnel?”

Charlie paused. Their tattooed escort shifted uncomfortably.

“No, I don’t remember.”

“Open the airlock,” Ehrich ordered. “We’re going to take another look.”

Instead of going to the airlock door, Jinn reached to his neck tattoo, and a real snake pulled free from his skin. This was no tattoo. He whipped the black cobra around by the tail at Ehrich. The fangs snapped the air just a hair's width away from Ehrich's eye. He threw himself back against the metal wall, while Charlie rushed the tattooed man. His partner slammed into Jinn's midsection knocking him down, but the cobra's tail coiled around Charlie's raised fist.

Ehrich launched from his position and caught the head of the snake before it could bite Charlie. The cobra's skin felt cold and slippery-smooth in his hands. As he struggled with the creature, Jinn grabbed Charlie by the throat. Ehrich forced the snake's head toward Jinn's face. His eyes widened as the fangs opened up at him.

"Where did the purple worker go?" Ehrich demanded.

"Not telling you anything," he grunted.

The snake snapped the air in front of his nose.

"Ehrich, let him have it."

"You heard my friend. One last chance to talk."

Jinn roared and bucked the pair off. Ehrich rolled to the side, letting go of the snake. The tattooed man put his head down and charged as Ehrich leapt up and set his feet. Then, at the last minute, Ehrich ducked. Misdirection was his friend and momentum was Jinn's enemy. He slammed head first into the wall and slumped to the floor, dazed. Ehrich sprinted over and kicked Jinn in the head to finish the job. The big man was out.

Ehrich then rushed to help Charlie who was trying to avoid the snake, now slithering along the floor. The snake lashed out at Charlie, who pulled his leg back just in time. Ehrich dove on the ground and grabbed the snake's tail. He flung it hard against the wall beside the unconscious tattooed man. It did not move again.

"I guess it's safe to assume that there's something here that they don't want us to see."

Ehrich nodded. "I'm sure that boneheaded demon wasn't in the tunnel, but what happened to him?"

"He walked into the airlock just before we had to go in. I remember that much."

"Me too," Ehrich said. He examined the walls. No other entrances, just the two they had used. The walls seemed solid.

"You remember that magic trick I told you about, Charlie? The disappearing rabbit?"

His friend nodded. "Yeah. So?"

"You want to know the secret?"

"Now? I think we have higher priorities, Ehrich."

"The secret was the box, Charlie. The magician showed the audience the box from the front, but not from the top where he put the rabbit in. The reason was pretty obvious once I saw inside. The box had two sections. One for the audience to see an empty space. The other for the rabbit to sit in. All the magician did was install a mirror so the box looked the right size."

"Thanks for telling me the secret, but what does it have to do with this?"

"The airlock. We're supposed to think there are only two ways in and out. What if there's more to it than meets the eye?"

He tapped the metal wall on one side of the airlock.

"Ehrich, if they needed a secret entrance, they'd have to hide it not only from us but from the other workers."

"Right. So, if you're going to work in the tunnel, which way are you looking?"

“The place you need to go. The other door.” Charlie pointed at the vault door.

“And what place aren’t you looking?” Ehrich asked.

Charlie turned around.

Ehrich smiled. The pair walked to the other end of the airlock and examined the vault door. Ehrich noticed a faint seam on the ground. He tapped his foot around the seam. The tapping sounded more hollow here than the other spots on the floor. He knelt and felt along the seam until he found a lip. He slid a large tile of the floor away to reveal a short drop to a passageway below.

Charlie smiled. “Houdini does it again.”

“Ta-da.”

Ehrich slid into the hole and Charlie followed into the narrow passageway. Light came from the far end of it. The heat was oppressive as the pair moved along the tunnel. Their footsteps echoed and they slowed down to silence their steps. Ahead, Ehrich could hear metal pounding against metal. He wondered if the Dimensionals were building a tunnel to somewhere else. He cycled through his memory of New York and tried to recall any important locations in the West Village. Gansevoort Market came to mind, but a place for merchants to sell their wares didn’t strike him as a target.

Charlie tugged Ehrich’s duster. “Don’t suppose you have a volt pistol up your sleeve.”

“Let’s see what’s at the end of the tunnel and decide what to do.”

“I vote for getting reinforcements.”

Ehrich shushed his friend and crept to the end of the tunnel. The light came from a forge well below the opening and far back against a vast cavern. The rocky walls reflected the orange glow throughout the space. Ehrich peered at the area below their position.

A dozen labourers worked at the forge. Most of the light was emitting from the burning furnace. The labourers were massive, but not as gigantic as the machines they worked on. In front of the forge, an army of iron, human-shaped exoskeletons stood at attention. These impressive armoured bodies easily stood three times the height of a man. Each unit had a cockpit for an operator. A thick weapons turret with multiple barrels around the perimeter adorned the iron arms of each exoskeleton unit.

The Dimensional with the bone-shard mohawk sat inside the cockpit of one of the machines. The massive contraption lifted its arm and aimed a weapon turret at the rock wall. Razor projectiles flew out of the barrels as the turret whirred around. The barrage left a gaping hole in the rock wall.

Ehrich and Charlie peered over the ledge at the squadron formation of exoskeleton machines. Affixed to the back of each of the iron suits of armour was a steam turbine. These servos operated the hydraulic limbs through a series of high-tension cables that were like a network of exterior nerves along the iron hides. Searchlights sat atop the dome-shaped helmets. A red-skinned labourer mounted a keg-shaped iron turret to one of the exoskeleton's tree trunk-like arms.

Charlie whispered to Ehrich, "There are at least five hundred of these things. What do you think they're for?"

"Maybe they make digging easier? I don't know. Maybe we should take a closer look."

Charlie hissed, "It's him."

"Who?"

"The kid who shot at you."

Ehrich crawled forward so he could get a better look. A dark-haired boy strode up to the workers and pointed at one of the exoskeletons. They rushed to do his bidding, skirting around him as if he were going to snap their heads off.

Ehrich's eyes widened in disbelief. Though the boy was older and a little taller than he remembered, there was no denying the thick eyebrows and the hooknose.

"Dash!" Ehrich gasped.

BROTHER FOUND, BROTHER LOST

Ehrich couldn't believe his eyes. The boy's hair was shorter and straight, but the bushy eyebrows that set the Weisz family apart from others remained thick. While this teen looked like his brother, the way he carried himself seemed nothing like the old Dash. When they lived in Wisconsin, he was a tag-along, always seeking Ehrich's approval before he took any action. He'd shuffle from foot to foot if he had to decide where to go. He'd play with his food on the plate, unable to decide what to eat first. This Dash was a leader. He commanded the attention and respect of the workers. Ehrich couldn't bring himself to believe this boy was his brother, and yet he couldn't deny the growing pit in his stomach as he felt shame for failing to search harder for Dash. He tried to tamp down the guilt now spreading across his chest and crushing the air out of his lungs.

"You know that kid?" Charlie asked.

"Yes. No. I'm not sure," Ehrich said.

"How?"

"It can't be him. It's impossible. I saw him die."

"You're not making sense, Ehrich. Who is he?"

"My brother."

"But he's a demon."

Ehrich stiffened, realizing he had said too much. "I mean, he looks like my brother. We should scout the area before we go."

Ehrich started down the incline. Dash's voice whispered in his mind. "*Ehrich*."

He hesitated.

"*No!*" His brother's voice said louder.

Ehrich silently counted to ten to drown out the voice.

"You okay?" Charlie asked.

"Yes. Go ahead." He motioned his partner to take the lead, then he followed.

"*Ehrich, don't go!*" Dash screamed in his mind. A chorus of voices joined Dash's warning. Ehrich's head reeled from the wall of sound. He staggered backwards.

Dash's doppelganger turned and pointed up. "Intruders!"

Charlie grabbed his friend by the arm and shouted, "We're done for. Out, out, out!"

He pulled Ehrich to the top of the incline and shoved him toward the tunnel. Ehrich had barely taken two steps before he skidded to a stop. The tattooed man careened toward them.

"I have the intruders!" he yelled.

Ehrich rushed at Jinn, but he was ready. He braced himself and caught the boy, pushing him back to the edge of the cliff. Ehrich's feet skidded across the surface as he tried to hold himself against this too-powerful opponent. Then Charlie rushed in and delivered a right hook to Jinn's jaw. The dazed man staggered away, but stayed on his feet.

"Take them! They can't leave!" Dash cried out.

The guards and workers charged up the steep incline. Charlie hauled Ehrich to his feet, but Jinn grabbed Ehrich's leg. Charlie swooped in and kicked the man in the chest, sending him rolling down the incline.

Ehrich and Charlie ran into the tunnel and reached the opening. Ehrich spotted a ladder against the wall and climbed up. Charlie followed. Once in the airlock, Ehrich leapt to the vault door and spun the wheel mechanism hard to the left until the large circular door hissed open. The teens bolted through the opening and pushed their backs against the giant airlock door, shoving it closed. Ehrich turned around and spun the lock wheel to the right until the door hissed shut. Charlie hurried to a large crate of picks and shovels at the end of the corridor. He grabbed three picks, then scrambled back to Ehrich, who gave the lock wheel one last hard crank.

"This will hold them off long enough for us to get out of here," Charlie said. He slid the handle of the pick into the spokes of the lock wheel. Then he gave one of the other picks to Ehrich.

The boys stepped back from the vault as the wheel began to turn by itself. The pick jammed against the mechanism and the lock wheel stayed in place. Whoever was on the other side would be stuck until the guard from the surface let them out. Ehrich planned on being long gone by the time that happened.

On the other side of the vault door, the Dimensional with the bone-shard mohawk strained at the wheel, trying to spin it open. His taut muscles glistened in the dim light, but brute force wasn't enough. Other labourers were gathered in the airlock behind the massive man.

The Dash doppelganger pushed through the crowd. He gnashed his teeth. "Enough, child. You will strain yourself and your body needs to be ready for the battle ahead."

The boy tested the wheel himself and turned around. Everyone looked down. "The next shift arrives in ten hours. That is when this door will open. By then, the intruders will have escaped. Unfortunate. I'm curious. Who allowed them to see our arsenal?"

A groan came from one side of the airlock. Workers roused the tattooed man and hauled him to his feet to face Dash.

"They were hunters, sir," he explained. "I had no choice."

"Unfortunate," the boy said again. His voice was low and menacing. He lifted his arm to reveal a crossbow strapped to the wrist. He took aim at the tattooed man's chest.

The mood suddenly shifted as an eerie calm filled the airlock and the workers bowed their heads and backed away. Dash turned and lowered his gaze instantly. A red-skinned giant climbed up from below. He wore a brilliant emerald robe that hung down to his feet. His jade tael was missing from around his neck, traded for his freedom.

"A frightened soldier will serve better than a dead one," Ba Tian pronounced, stroking his ivory tusks.

Dash lowered the crossbow and nodded.

Ehrich and Charlie climbed the ladders, ascending to the surface. As soon as Charlie cleared the first one, Ehrich pushed the ladder off so that any surface rescuers would have trouble getting down. He ran around the ledge, kicking the other ladders down, as Charlie headed to the next level. Then Ehrich went up, while Charlie did the same with the ladders on the next level.

When they finally reached the top, the gate guard spotted them. At first, he raised an eyebrow, searching for his partner. He scratched his bushy umber beard. Once he noticed that the two teens were wielding picks, however, the situation finally clicked in his brain, and he drew a long knife with serrated edges.

"Charlie, flank him," Ehrich said.

His friend hunched low, waving the pick back and forth to test the weight. Ehrich moved to the right, putting distance between himself and Charlie. The gate guard would have to choose one of them. He opted for Ehrich.

He charged with the knife high over his head. Ehrich raised his pick with both hands to block the downward blow, but he left his midsection open. The burly man kicked him square in the gut and sent him flying backward. Though the man was big, he moved with deceptive speed.

Charlie rushed at the guard from behind, swinging his pick at the back of the man's head. He ducked as the dirt-encrusted pick whistled over him. Charlie had expected to connect and the miss threw him off balance. He staggered two steps to the left, exposing his side.

The gate guard slashed and sliced through Charlie's duster. A seasoned hunter, the boy let his momentum carry him forward to roll away from the blade. The bearded man lunged at him, raising his blade for a killing blow. Charlie spun around and drove the pick into his attacker's thigh. Instead of striking flesh and bone, Charlie smacked the impenetrable iron hide of a prosthetic leg. The pick handle broke in half.

The gate guard quickly took advantage of Charlie's surprise and drove the serrated blade at Charlie's abdomen, but the swift hunter angled his body and the blade only nicked him. He slammed his forearm into the guard's wrist, knocking the knife out of the man's hand.

"Not so tough now, are we?" Charlie taunted, advancing.

The guard backed up and set his feet. Charlie lunged, and the man kicked him in the stomach. Then the guard grabbed Charlie by the back of the hair and drove the boy's head into his metal knee. The crunch of bone against metal was sickening. Charlie's limp form crumpled to the ground. The guard raised his metal leg to crush Charlie's head.

"No!" Ehrich hooked the handle of his pick around the guard's neck and hauled him away from his injured friend. The guard drove his legs back, throwing himself and Ehrich toward the edge of the quarry pit. Ehrich dropped the pick as he rolled toward the edge and then over. For a second, he was floating in mid air, trying to distinguish ground from sky. He shot his arm out and grabbed the edge. His body slammed into the rocky wall and he was momentarily stunned.

Towering above him, the bearded man with the iron leg turned the pick in his ham hock hands and eyed the helpless Weisz. He raised the pick over his head and brought it down on the boy. Ehrich threw his other hand up to grasp the ledge and angled himself to the side. The pick drove into the rock. Ehrich looked down. The drop was too far. He'd most likely break his neck if he let go. He could feel his fingers slipping. He grunted as he tried to reposition his hands.

The big man freed the pick and took aim for another deadly blow. He hoisted the makeshift weapon high in the air. Ehrich knew this was the end. He shut his eyes.

Crack!

A rush of wind whipped past Ehrich's head. He opened his eyes and looked down. The bearded man's twisted form lay sprawled out on the ground, two tiers down. The man's eyes stared vacantly up at the sky.

Above, a wobbly Charlie stood on the ledge clutching a plank of wood.

"Not bad," Ehrich said. "Want to give me a hand?"

His friend dropped the plank and bent down to help Ehrich up. Once his friend was safe, Charlie sat and put his head in his hands.

"Are you all right?" Ehrich asked.

"Ma hea is thwobbing," Charlie said, slurring his words.

A nasty lump formed on his friend's forehead where the guard had kneed him, but there seemed to be no other injuries.

"Can you stand, Charlie?"

The teen tried, but his legs shook and Ehrich had to steady him. Charlie then doubled over and vomited.

"We have to get you to the surgeon," Ehrich said.

He picked up the guard's serrated blade, threw his friend's arm over his neck and headed to the street.

The teens put some distance between the tunnel project and themselves. Ehrich stopped a few blocks away to get a better grip on his friend. Charlie was losing consciousness.

"Erie, why didna ya... ell me...? Er brother?"

"Save your energy, Charlie."

"Demon..." he mumbled as his head rolled to one side.

Ehrich yanked on his friend's arm, keeping him awake. Out of the corner of his eye, he caught a figure darting quickly from cover. At first, he thought the tunnel workers had broken out of the airlock and caught up with them, but then he recognized Wilhelm.

"I see him! He's got Charlie." Wilhelm cried out, pointing.

Though he was not fond of Wilhelm, Ehrich was still glad to see him—until his former squad mate raised his volt pistol.

"You're under arrest," Wilhelm said.

ENTER PURGATORY

"Wilhelm, what are you doing? It's me," Ehrich said.

"Of course I know it's you, *Houdini,*" the German teen sneered. "Commander Farrier told us how you set the demon free. You're a traitor to Demon Watch."

Ehrich glanced at Charlie, who was fading into unconsciousness. What Charlie needed was medical attention. What chance would he have of surviving if he was branded an accomplice to a fugitive? His career as a hunter would effectively be over, even if he survived. Ehrich couldn't be responsible for that.

"Houdini, you and your pal have nowhere to run," Wilhelm said, "so you might as well give up now."

He lifted the serrated blade to his friend's throat and yelled, "One step further and Charlie gets it!"

His friend weakly struggled against his grip. "Wha—?"

"This is my hostage, Wilhelm. Put your gun down and I'll let him go."

Wilhelm hesitated.

Then Margaret and Gino arrived on the scene. "Let Charlie go!" shouted Margaret.

The squad was only tracking him. Charlie wasn't a target. If Ehrich was going to keep his friend safe, he'd have make sure everyone thought Charlie was still on their side.

He shouted, "I will gut him right before your eyes. You want that on your conscience, Wilhelm? Gino? Your choice, Margaret. What will it be?"

The trio whispered to each other.

Charlie gasped, "Ehrich?"

"Shut up," he barked. "You want to live?"

"Leggo."

"Not until they drop their guns. Last chance, Wilhelm!"

"We have orders to bring you in," Wilhelm said. "Dead or alive."

Gino corrected him. "Farrier didn't say that. He said just bring him in."

"Shut it," Wilhelm snapped.

Ehrich pressed the blade against Charlie's neck. Margaret lowered her volt pistol. Gino did the same. Wilhelm shook his head until Margaret punched him in the arm. "Put it down. Now!"

He obeyed.

"Now step back," Ehrich ordered.

They retreated.

"They'll get you the help you need," Ehrich whispered. Then he pushed his friend to the ground and ran away.

"The fugitive is moving down Morton Street," Wilhelm yelled.

Ehrich glanced back. His former squad mates were gathered around the fallen Charlie, but just a block away four new hunters were coming toward the group. He sped across the busy lanes, dodging horse-drawn carriages and ducking past curious gawkers. A few blocks away, he found himself under the Ninth Avenue line.

The four hunters had fresh legs and were gaining ground. Ehrich had no choice but to fight. He slowed to catch his breath. He leaned against the iron support of the elevated railroad, pressing his back against the pillar, feeling the rivet heads press into his shoulder. The hunters surrounded him. Their teslatron rifles were raised and ready to shoot. He recognized the freckled face of Lilith, the leader of Farrier's top squad.

"You're under arrest for treason," she said. "Hands up."

Ehrich rolled on the balls of his feet, his gaze shifting from side to side to pick out the most likely target.

"He's uncooperative," Lilith said. "Shoot him."

Ehrich pushed off from the girder and dove at the legs of the scrawny black-haired teen to his right. A bolt of energy seared the air just over his head. A near miss. He grappled with the teen, knowing that the others wouldn't shoot with a comrade in close proximity. He eyed Lilith as she swung her rifle around, and he angled his opponent between the two of them.

Then a stocky hunter grabbed Ehrich's hair and swung him around, slamming the side of his face into the pillar. Ehrich felt a hard punch to his kidney, sending waves of pain up his back. The hunter slammed Ehrich's head into the pillar again, cutting his lip. He pulled his head back for a third smash but stopped and released his grip on Ehrich's hair.

Ehrich heard a low, menacing growl as he staggered against

the metal pillar. The German shepherd from Mr. Serenity's Museum of Curiosities stood a few feet away from the group, baring its teeth. Flanking it, a pack of huge dogs padded toward the hunters. Lilith backed up, raising her rifle.

"Back," she said.

The other hunters raised their rifles and took aim. The dogs still advanced. Lilith fired at a pit bull, to no effect. The dogs closed the gap. More shots filled the air, but not a single dog fell. Lilith turned and ran. Her squad mates scattered as the dogs split from their pack and chased after them. Barking faded in the distance.

Alone, Ehrich slid to the ground, trying to figure out which part of him hurt the most. He tested his bloody lip and reached behind to massage his bruised back. Nothing was broken, but he would be sore for days. At the sound of a short bark, he looked up and met the unflinching gaze of Mr. Serenity's German shepherd.

The dog padded up to where Ehrich was sitting until they were nose to nose. For a second, he half-expected the mutt to chew off his face. Then he noticed its leather collar; more specifically, the pearl cameo attached to the collar. As Ehrich reached up to touch the cameo, the dog trotted away, but then turned to look back expectantly.

Ehrich didn't know when Lilith and her squad might return, so he decided to follow. The shepherd led him away from the elevated trains, past shop owners and refined shoppers along the wide avenue. They travelled for nearly an hour until they had made it to the east side of Manhattan, beyond the Bowery but before the wharfs. The dog stopped near a gangly merchant, hawking cooked yams. Easily, this man could have been one of the attractions in the Museum of Curiosities as the tallest man in New York. He turned to Ehrich then gazed down at the dog.

"Are you absolutely certain?"

The dog barked.

The tall man rolled his cart out of the way to reveal cellar doors. He stooped over and pulled up the metal cellar doors. They clanked against the stone sidewalk. He beckoned Ehrich toward the hole. The boy glanced into the hole and saw nothing.

A pair of hands shoved him hard from behind and he toppled into the inky darkness. The fall abruptly ended when Ehrich landed on a smooth glass floor. He found himself in a tiny round compartment barely large enough for himself and the dog that landed beside him. Behind him was a bench, and before him was an instrument panel of gauges and dials. The dog slammed its paw on a button on the panel and the vehicle lurched forward. The transport slid toward a large glass pneumatic tube. Ehrich shot back into the bench from the sudden acceleration.

They flew through the tube at a blistering pace, zigzagging through the rock, always moving downwards. Ehrich clutched his mouth, trying to keep from throwing up. The dog cocked its head to one side and watched Ehrich, seemingly oblivious to the jolting descent. After an eternity, the vehicle slowed and came out at the top end of an enormous cavern. The vehicle's top lights snapped on, revealing an alien landscape of stalagmites and stalactites. How far beneath Manhattan they were, Ehrich had no clue. The clear pneumatic tube joined a network of other clear tubes, all leading toward a massive globe hovering between the stalactites and stalagmites, like a ball held in the teeth of a giant monster.

Glowing rings rotated around the globe, illuminating the city within. Glass towers rose from the surface and nearly touched the glowing rings. Golden minarets dotted the cityscape, which teemed with people moving through pneumatic tubes between the buildings. His vehicle whizzed toward the centre of the city.

"What is this place?" he asked himself.

"It's Purgatory," a girl's voice answered.

He turned around, but only the dog sat beside him. He examined the panel of instruments for a speaker.

"Who said that? Where are you?"

"Right here," said the dog.

"You can talk? Impossible. Okay, now I'm talking to a dog. I think I'm losing my mind. No, now I'm talking to myself. I *know* I'm losing my mind."

The cameo on the dog's choker flashed a brilliant emerald green and suddenly, in place of the dog, Amina appeared. He stared at her vibrant, ebony face, slack-jawed with wonder.

"How did you do that?" Ehrich asked.

She smiled enigmatically and said nothing.

"What do you want with me? Where are we going?"

"In good time, but first..." She knifed her hand into his shirt and yanked the medallion from around his neck.

"Hey, how did you know?"

"I was in the Museum when you showed up that first time."

"No, you weren't."

"Ruff."

"Oh."

She examined the chimera image, running her finger over the smooth metal. "Where did you find this?"

"You know what the image means?" Ehrich asked.

"I'm asking the questions. Where did you find this?"

Ehrich refused to answer. "I'm not telling you anything until I get some answers of my own. What does the chimera mean?"

The vehicle came to a stop inside one of the minarets. Amina pushed open the hatch and stepped out. She motioned Ehrich to follow.

"Where are we going?" he asked.

"Follow me if you want those answers."

The corridor was see-through, allowing Ehrich to observe the road below. Unlike the brownstone that dominated New York, glass seemed to be the primary material used in construction down here. But it was nothing like the glass he had seen. The material here was smoother and denser, and some was even opaque. Above, the rotating rings orbited the floating complex and illuminated the city.

Amina strode across the glass floor, creating the illusion that she was walking on air. Ehrich stepped behind her gingerly. He navigated the glass corridor and finally found himself on more solid-looking surroundings. Ahead of him, strange designs in the smooth obsidian floor lit up with Amina's every step, lighting a path to a circular doorway at the far end of the hallway. Ehrich followed.

She placed the palm of her hand on the door's centre and a red glow spread across the silver door, which spiralled open like an iris.

They stepped into a round room covered with dusty books and uncomfortable-looking church pews. In the middle of the room, Mr. Serenity was examining the tome Ehrich had first seen Amina carry into Demon Gate.

"Where am I?" he demanded.

Amina crossed over to where Mr. Serenity was standing and handed him the medallion she'd taken from around Ehrich's neck. "I'm going to need your help, Mr. Serenity. He won't talk."

"Maybe you didn't ask nicely."

"No, he's stubborn."

"I suspect he's probably bewildered."

"Hello? Someone please tell me what's going on here!"

Mr. Serenity smiled. "You look like a man who could use something to drink. Sorry to say all I have is tea. Will that do?"

Ehrich shook his head.

"Tea will settle your nerves. Let me pour you a cup. What's your name?"

"Ehrich. Ehrich Weisz."

Mr. Serenity poured a cup of tea for him. He then poured one for Amina.

"Now, I'm sure all of this may be a bit overwhelming, but let me put your mind at ease. We don't mean you any ill will. We simply want to know how you came about this device."

"Tell me what the medallion means first."

"See, Mr. Serenity?" Amina said. "I told you. If we delay any longer, we're going to—"

"In good time. Drink up, son. Don't be rude."

Ehrich picked up the cup. The tea smelled of mint and rosemary. He only meant to take one sip, but he drank half in two swallows.

"Mr. Serenity, what do you think about using the hypermnesium?"

He waved her off. "Let's try talking first, shall we?" He turned to Ehrich. "I'll put this as simply as I can, son. You have something which comes from our world. Amina is so curious to learn how you got it. Her urgency has made her forget her manners. Can you tell us where you got it, so that we, in turn, might be able to help you?" He winked at Amina. "See, that's not that hard, is it?"

"He hasn't answered you yet," she shot back.

Ehrich didn't know if he could trust these two, but this was the closest he had ever come to getting answers about the medallion. "It belonged—belongs—to my brother."

Mr. Serenity cracked a wide grin at Amina. She clammed up.

"I don't know how he got it. That's what I've been trying to find out. In the tunnel, he didn't act like himself. Maybe the medallion had some kind of effect on him."

"Ah. You wonder if your brother was really your brother," Mr. Serenity deduced.

"Yes. You have devices that can change her into a dog."

Amina smiled. "Woof."

Mr. Serenity chuckled. "Son, what Amina does is an illusion. She has a device that projects what she wants you to see. She prefers the German shepherd. Why is that, Amina?"

"Everyone loves a dog," she said.

"This medallion does the same thing?" Ehrich asked.

The purple-haired man examined the trinket in his hands. He studied the double loop of the gear wheels and the smaller gear wheels within them that created the impression the mechanism extended to infinity.

"I don't know what this device does, but if you'll permit me, I can do some analysis."

"Can you explain why my brother had it?"

"Perhaps. Do you want me to try?"

"Go ahead," Ehrich said. At last, he might find the answers

he'd sought for two years.

"It will take some time. Amina, perhaps you can show our guest around while he waits. Perhaps even ask him some questions... nicely."

She grimaced. Mr. Serenity left with the medallion, leaving the two alone. Awkward silence filled the room as Amina stared at him.

He finally broke the silence. "That device you brought to this dimension. We opened it."

"The electrical man?"

"Who? What? Oh. Yes, the electrical man. His name is Nikola Tesla. What is the device for?"

She changed the subject. "You must be hungry. Come, let's get you something to eat. Please."

Amina led Ehrich out of the chamber and into Purgatory's streets. The air revived Ehrich. The pedestrians streaming past him seemed to multiply as they hustled past the shiny glass walls that reflected their images. The pavement appeared to be constructed of similar smoked glass material. Through the tinted surface, Ehrich viewed a lower road with more people hurrying past other tall structures. He wasn't sure if this was the next tier of Purgatory or if this were some kind of reflection.

The raven-haired girl took Ehrich by the arm and guided him through the crowd of Dimensionals. Few of them looked like Amina or Mr. Serenity.

"What happened to your people?" he asked.

"There is a marketplace in the city square. We may find umami beans today if we are fortunate."

"Sure. Is this what your world looks like?"

"Purgatory? No, this is a hybrid of worlds. It's designed to make the survivors feel at ease."

"So Purgatory isn't just for your people."

She fell silent as they stepped onto a flight of moving stairs that descended to the lower level. He gripped the railing to keep from teetering on the moving steps. He watched the other denizens of Purgatory walk past. Ehrich realized they were mostly refugees like him, travellers from different dimensions, orphaned by circumstances beyond their control. For the first time in two years, he felt like he was among his own, and part of him wanted to confess the truth to Amina.

"Where is your family? Are they here?"

She didn't answer his question. Instead, she said, "You must love your brother very much to go through all this."

Ehrich's face flushed as he thought of all the time he'd wasted, having abandoned his search for Dash for so long. "I would do anything for him."

"What was he like?" she asked.

"Why do you want to know?"

"I like hearing about families," Amina said.

Ehrich had spent two years pretending to be an orphan, avoiding any talk about his brother or his parents. He'd had to play a part, and a little bit of him died every time he pretended his family didn't exist. Now that he suddenly didn't have to hide this part of his life, he felt freer than he had ever been.

"He followed me everywhere and tried to imitate all the things I did. At first, I wanted him to leave me alone, but our mother had given me instructions to look after him. And I did. I had dreams of being a high-wire artist. I tied a rope between two trees and practiced. As soon as I jumped off, he jumped on. I dared him to go across. Well, he tried. Not successfully.

He fell on his arm. I thought he'd broken it, but he just stood up and took a bow. The kids watching—they laughed. Dash, he laughed along with them. That was my brother. He had a way with people. What about you? What about your family?"

Amina turned away. "We're almost at the marketplace. Are you hungry?"

He shook his head. "Tell me something about your family. What about your people?"

"They are gone," she answered, her lips thinned as she walked ahead.

Ehrich pushed the issue. "Wait. Isn't Piotravisk one of your people?"

"No, he is a refugee from another sector. How do you know him?"

"I found him when I was looking for you on Devil's Island. He showed me how you two met. Do you know Ole Lukoje? Nasty creature with metal talons. Likes eyes."

She stopped at a vendor's stall and picked up a purple banana. She paid for it and walked along the busy street of vendors.

"That is his name? We've crossed paths before in other sectors. I would not say I know him, but I know his type."

"What were you both doing in that dimension?" Ehrich asked.

She peeled the purple banana to reveal the lime-green fruit inside. She took a bite and walked along the marketplace of multi-dimensional vendors and shoppers. "In the aftermath of war, there are two types of people. Those who rush toward the fallen to give aid, and those who slink in to profit. This Ole Lukoje was not the only one to take advantage of the situation, though he is particularly nasty. He prefers fresh eyes."

Ehrich nodded. "Why do you risk your life for strangers?"

“Because others have done the same for me. If not for Mr. Serenity, I would have been...” she trailed off. She stopped at a stall with an array of skewered barbecued bats. “They are quite delicious. You want one?” She paid for one and bit into the batwing, then offered Ehrich a piece.

He waved off her offer. “What would have happened?”

She pointed at her mouth, indicating she was unable to answer, but Ehrich suspected she was unwilling to answer. He let the matter drop. Everyone was entitled to a few secrets.

A REMINDER OF HOME

Ehrich slept in Mr. Serenity's quarters, while the portly man examined the medallion all through the night. The next morning, Ehrich dined with Amina, tasting an exotic golden brown bread she called Xibanic. The wheat grew in a section of Purgatory called Orion. The bakers in Purgatory milled the grains into a savoury flour that, when baked, tasted like nothing he had ever eaten before. Maybe the tangy zest of a lemon and the rich flavour of a lobster together would come close, but Ehrich couldn't get enough of the bread.

Ehrich wanted to know more about Amina. She didn't like talking about herself much, which left Ehrich to drive much of the conversation. He decided to talk about Nikola Tesla, his mentor. "He's a bit like Mr. Serenity, but not as fleshy. He has the weirdest thing that he does. Everything has to be in threes. He groups his equipment in three piles. He counts three steps at a time. He even divides his food into threes."

"Why does he do that?"

Ehrich shrugged. "I think counting helps him organize everything."

"Even food? How does he do that?"

"I saw him at lunch once. He cut his sandwich in half, then cut each half into three pieces. He wrapped one half and put it away, then proceeded to eat each third that was out."

"Let me guess, in three bites."

Ehrich laughed. "Yes. Isn't that the oddest thing?"

She nodded. "Mr. Serenity can top that. He doesn't even know he does it, but when he concentrates, he wets his lips then licks his nose."

"How can he do that?"

"Mr. Serenity has a tongue that's this long." Amina held her hands about a foot apart.

"What is he? Part lizard?"

Amina cocked her head to the side. "Yes. Yes, he is."

Embarrassed, Ehrich tried to backpedal until Amina began to laugh. "You're too easy, Ehrich Weisz."

They finished eating and cleared the dishes. Mr. Serenity was so engrossed in examining the medallion he didn't even come out to eat. The pair settled back at the table.

Ehrich asked, "If that medallion is from your dimension, do you think it could have done something to Dash? Taken over his mind?"

"No. Our devices alter perception or manipulate appearances. My people had strict ethical laws about how our technology was used. Taking over someone's mind was like, well, it was something akin to slavery. This crime was punishable by exile."

"There has to be some explanation for why my brother was acting so strangely."

"Don't worry, Ehrich. Mr. Serenity will unlock the medallion's secret."

Ehrich nodded and settled back in his chair. "Tell me more about what your people are like."

A dark look fell over Amina's face, but she looked away, reaching for the golden brown loaf on the table.

"Do you want more Xibanic?" she asked, cutting a slice. The ensuing silence was thicker than the slab of bread she sawed.

"You know what I could really eat right now? Apple pie."

She shrugged. "What is that?"

"An apple is a fruit that grows in this dimension. You can bake apples in a pastry shell for the sweetest thing you've ever tried. The best apple pie is the one my mother bakes. I could eat two of them right now. One time, my mother locked a fresh-baked pie in a cupboard so Dash and I wouldn't get our hands on it, but the pie smelled so good, we broke into the cupboard. We couldn't resist it."

This was the first time Ehrich had managed to pick a lock. Necessity was the mother of invention, and he was desperate for the apple pie. He didn't so much pick the lock as he loosened the moorings and broke the cupboard door. Now, he salivated at the memory of biting through the flaky crust and tasting the sweet apples. He smiled at the memory of Dash, his face covered with the evidence of pie, protesting their innocence. His eyes welled at the memories of home.

"There are things about home that you can't find anywhere else. When you're home, you feel like nothing can ever go wrong. It's like—" He stopped when he saw Amina wiping her own eyes.

"What's wrong?"

She shook her head. "It's nothing."

"Something happened to your family," Ehrich said. "I can guess that much. Will you tell me?"

"My family is no more."

"What happened to them?"

Their old companion, silence, joined them, but only for a moment. "In your language, you would call it the apocalypse," Amina said in hushed tones. "That is what happened to my world. The end of things. A warlord came to us with his troops, and without warning, he massacred everyone. My family. Friends. Everyone. My world wasn't the only one. This warlord has orphaned many of the people in Purgatory. With his armies, he moves from one realm to another. Some say he journeys from world to world to seize resources. Some say he does it to feed his starving people. Others say he is simply mad for power. The only thing people know for sure is that he leaves nothing but ruin in his path."

"What do you believe?"

"I think he's a divine punishment for the scientists opening the portals. We were not meant to go to other worlds because of warlords like Ba Tian."

Ehrich stiffened. "Ba Tian?"

"Yes."

"You're sure?"

She nodded.

Ehrich said, "I've seen him. On Devil's Island."

"Ba Tian is here? We have to tell Mr. Serenity."

"Why?" Ehrich asked.

"He only travels to the dimensions he wishes to conquer."

Ehrich recalled the exoskeleton units he had seen in the tunnel. They weren't just powerful excavation machines; they were weapons of war.

THE HYPERMNESIUM

Mr. Serenity was hunched over a table examining the medallion when Amina and Ehrich burst into his lab. He nearly dropped the trinket on the floor in surprise.

"Mr. Serenity! Ba Tian has set up base here in this dimension. Ehrich has seen the war machines."

"What? Tell me. Everything."

Ehrich recounted his experience with the warlord in Ninth Circle and described the machines he had found under the Hudson River. Mr. Serenity probed Ehrich about the contraptions. How many were there? What armaments did they have? Meanwhile, Amina paced, becoming more and more agitated.

"We have to prepare for battle," she said.

Mr. Serenity agreed. "I can see why he wants this dimension. Demon Gate is one of the most stable portals that exists. He could send his army to any dimension from here. The universe would become an open road to him."

"We must stop him before he destroys any other worlds," Amina said.

Mr. Serenity agreed. "We'll amass our forces in Purgatory, but we don't stand a chance unless we can contact Ning Shu."

"I'm sure she'll reach out again."

"Hold on, hold on," Ehrich interrupted. "You were supposed to help me figure out what happened to my brother."

"I'm sorry, son, but I don't know what this medallion does. The technology is beyond anything I've ever seen. With more time and better equipment, maybe I could determine the purpose, but your guess is as good as mine."

"Not good enough," Ehrich said. "After all, he's a part of this uprising, too. We should at least figure out how he's connected!"

Mr. Serenity shook his head. "I'm at a loss; this is the best answer I can give you, I'm afraid. Amina, let's see the Kinetoscopic Codex. Maybe we can get a sense of what weapon she has that can defeat Ba Tian."

Amina rushed out.

"Mr. Serenity, please listen to me. It's important I find out about my brother."

Mr. Serenity fixed a gaze on him. "Son, if we fail against Ba Tian, the truth won't matter."

Amina returned with the book device. She placed it on the table and opened the cover. The image of the red-skinned Dimensional appeared again.

"Play the message," Mr. Serenity said.

Amina pressed a sequence of nubs on the inner workings of the book. The image of the crimson girl began to speak. "Mr. Serenity, the two of us share the same goals. The only difference is you lack the means of accomplishing your goal. I'm willing to share if you're willing to meet." The image froze.

"We could send another message to Ning Shu," Amina said.

"We've already sent three since she missed our meeting. Something must have happened to her."

"How do you know you can trust her?" Ehrich asked.

"That is the daughter of Ba Tian. She risked everything to betray her father," Mr. Serenity answered.

"His daughter? That's why they have the same jade tael. You don't think this is some kind of setup?"

He shook his head. "She has given us valuable information for some time now. Amina?"

She pressed another button and the screen image dissolved into a montage of battle scenes, in which red-skinned warriors decimated armies. Sequence after sequence of bloody war flashed across the screen. Some of the battles took place on land, others at sea; one was in the air. Red-skinned warriors in exoskeleton machines battled weaker forces, wiping them out. The machines looked exactly like the ones in the Hudson River tunnel.

She said, "Thanks to Ning Shu, we've learned some of her father's tactical moves. They've helped us win two battles. If Ning Shu has something that can help, we believe her."

"Then maybe I can help. I know where she is," Ehrich said.

"How do you know?"

"I saw her trying to get into your museum. She had a companion with her—a man—but when they spotted us, they ran."

Amina's eyes widened. "You're the reason we lost contact?"

"I can tell you where she went."

Mr. Serenity grabbed Ehrich's arm. "Tell us. Our future depends on this."

Ehrich shook his head. "*My* future depends on finding out the truth about my brother. Tell me what the medallion does, and I will lead you to Ning Shu."

"We don't know and we don't have time to figure it out," Amina argued.

"Then you'd better hurry."

Mr. Serenity shook his head. "I've exhausted all my resources."

"Amina said something about a hyper… hyper…"

She answered, "Hypermnesium.

"Yes. What about that?'

Amina turned to Mr. Serenity. "If he can help us win the war, we have to try."

"It's dangerous for the boy," the man said. "I don't want to take that kind of risk."

"What's the danger?" Ehrich asked.

Mr. Serenity fixed a look on the dark-haired boy. "The hypermnesium culls your memories and zeroes in on details you may not remember. Everything you've ever witnessed in your life is locked in your brain, but how you interpret what you see determines what you remember. This device allows us to see everything, not just the memories that matter to you. Your interactions with your brother may give us a clue to the nature of his medallion or his true origins. But the mind is a fragile thing. You could regress to the mental age of two if things go wrong."

"But if it works, you may learn what really happened to my brother?" Ehrich asked.

The round man nodded. "There are no guarantees."

"I'll take the risk."

"You're sure?"

"Positive."

"Very well." Mr. Serenity turned to Amina. "Help him relax and clear his mind of everything but his brother. I will prepare the hypermnesium."

An hour later, Ehrich sat down in a leather chair, and silver restraints automatically locked his arms in place. Amina patted him on the shoulder and assured him he would be fine, but he could see doubt in her green eyes.

"Ignore any memories that don't involve Dash," she said. "That apple pie you told me about. Picture yourself sharing the pie with your brother if you are ever in doubt. Always go back to this memory. Understand?"

He nodded as he leaned back in the chair. A black shade perched atop the large open cabinet of the hypermnesium. Silhouetted shapes were carved into the stiff material. A bulb projected light through the shade's geometric patterns and cast shadows on the walls. A massive pipe organ with rows of black and white keys sat beside the cabinet.

"We'll start with a little test," Mr. Serenity said as he placed a glass globe over Ehrich's head and attached wires to his forehead. "My world's musicologists learned certain combinations of notes can open neural pathways. All you have to do is play the right ones."

He pressed his fingers on the keys, and the black shade on the cabinet began to revolve as the light within came to life.

A tuneless melody filled the room.

"Your mother's hair was long and purple," Mr. Serenity said.

"What?"

He repeated the statement.

"No. It wasn't."

Ehrich tried to picture his mother, and an image of a blue jay appeared on the wall. This was the bird that perched on the window outside his dormitory bed on Devil's Island. The one he fed crumbs to every morning.

"This is not a good sign, Amina. The music usually conjures images of loved ones."

She turned to Ehrich. "The story you told me about stealing the pie. Concentrate on this memory."

He took a deep breath. Mr. Serenity played again.

The image of Dash appeared; he sat at the kitchen table with crumbs all over his lips. He denied eating the pie to their mother. This was not the hardened Dash doppelganger Ehrich saw amid the exoskeleton machines, but the doting brother who adored Ehrich so much he imitated his every gesture. On the wall, ahead of him, the projection of his memory appeared. The image switched to another memory; now, his brother balanced on the makeshift high wire between two trees. Ehrich stiffened as Dash fell on the ground. He closed his eyes, and the image shattered like a broken mirror into shards of other memories.

"Remember the apple pie," Amina said.

Mr. Serenity played another series of notes. A new set of images flashed on the wall. Dash donning a new cap in the apartment belonging to his parents. His father scolding Ehrich. A disappearing handkerchief. A marble inside a chalk circle.

"Now focus on the medallion. Did you ever see Dash with it?"

Amina's voice cut through the fog of images like the blast of a lighthouse horn.

"The medallion?"

"Yes. The one with the chimera."

"I like ice cream."

Mr. Serenity's voice drifted on the edges. "His mind is starting to fragment, Amina. We can't continue."

"Ehrich, listen to the sound of my voice. Do you remember the medallion that your brother wore?"

"I'm trying."

Mr. Serenity handed Amina the medallion. "Sense memory may help."

"Hold this, Ehrich." She pressed the medallion into his right hand. The images on the wall exploded into slashes of multi-coloured light. A thousand voices shouted in his mind. The images splintered into scenes of green-skinned Dimensionals falling before giant iron exoskeleton machines. Then an ocean world where gilled women gasped on a beach. They made no sense to Ehrich at all.

"Ehrich, focus on the pie. Your brother is eating the apple pie."

He tried to focus on the memory of sharing the pie with his brother, shutting out the alien images fighting for space in his memory. On the wall, the images finally coalesced into a cemetery. Was it the one on Devil's Island? No, it sharpened into the country graveyard where Ehrich had last seen his brother. Dash flicked on the device that opened the gateway into New York. He turned to face Ehrich but in this image, his eyes were dark and menacing.

Mr. Serenity gasped. "He's a Dimensional."

"What?" Amina asked.

"Look. That's a portal," he said.

A flurry of images followed. The portal, alien landscapes, his brother, the fight. The medallion slipping out of Dash's shirt and into Ehrich's hand. For an instant, a different face superimposed itself over Dash's cherubic face. The ethereal face belonged to a man with deep-set eyes and a crooked mouth. His eyes were cold and black as he stared ahead.

Then the image switched to the fight in the Bowery. Dash rushed into the crowd and staggered back with a knife in his belly. The images on the wall disintegrated into tiny points of light. Ehrich's body arched as he screamed.

Mr. Serenity tore the electrodes from Ehrich's head. "Look at me. Concentrate on my face. Shut everything else out. Breathe and keep your eyes on me."

Finally, his vision settled and he could focus on reality once more. Mr. Serenity unstrapped the restraints.

Amina asked, "Why didn't you tell us the truth?"

Ehrich opened his mouth to answer, but he vomited instead. He tried to stand up, but everything seemed to be spinning. All he could see was the floor rushing up to meet his face; then nothing but darkness.

When Ehrich awoke, he had no idea of how much time had passed. He rested on a divan in Mr. Serenity's study. He stared up at the constellation map on the ceiling and for a second he thought he was under the night sky. The clattering sound of a cup of tea beside him broke through his reverie, an offer from Amina.

"Feeling better, Ehrich?" she asked.

"Dizzy. Headache. Oh."

"Sorry," Mr. Serenity said. "The pain will go away eventually."

Amina crossed her arms. "You should have told us the truth. Were you ashamed?"

"I didn't know how."

Mr. Serenity patted Ehrich's hand. "Or maybe she didn't ask nicely."

Amina sniffed indignantly and walked away.

Ehrich propped himself up with a shoulder. "Did it work? What did you find out?"

"I think I know what the medallion is," Mr. Serenity said.

Ehrich asked, "What?"

"If what we saw on the hypermnesium is accurate, this is the Infinity Coil."

"I don't know what that is. What does it mean?" Ehrich asked.

"It means your brother is here," he answered, tapping the medallion.

"Impossible," Amina said. "That's only in legend."

"And like long-lasting legends, the story is likely based in some truth," Mr. Serenity proposed.

"Someone want to tell me what this is?" Ehrich asked.

Mr. Serenity motioned Amina to sit. "This is a piece of technology from the Fallen Age, when our scientists pursued knowledge without a thought to consequences or conscience. They created weapons of mass destruction. They experimented with the genetic code of humanity. They explored the fabric of existence. It was rumoured that the sum total of all their knowledge led to the invention of this device, the Infinity Coil."

Ehrich raised an eyebrow. "In English, please."

"Imagine a soul catcher which allows the user to replace the essence of a person with his own."

"You mean so they can take control of a person's body?"

Mr. Serenity nodded. "Not just the body, but the memories and personality."

Amina shifted in her seat. "According to legend, an assassin used the coil to jump from one body to another in order to carry out political murders."

"They called him Kifo, but no one knows his true name or his original form," Mr. Serenity added.

"My grandmother used to tell this story to scare us when we were little. How can this be true? He would have to be ancient by now," Amina said.

"This is why the Infinity Coil is so dangerous. The user can be immortal as long as he captures souls and uses their bodies. Ehrich, I believe Kifo has taken your brother's essence and assumed his body as his own."

"All those times I heard his voice, I thought they were my memories taunting me."

Amina's eyes widened. "You can hear your brother?"

Ehrich nodded. "What does it mean? Does it mean he's alive?"

"I can't be sure about this," Mr. Serenity said. "I think he's alive in a manner of speaking. His body is here on this plane, but the essence which makes him your brother is somewhere inside the Infinity Coil. Who knows how many other souls are trapped in here?"

"Then get him out!" For the first time, Ehrich felt more than just dread when he thought of his brother. He felt hope. He could save Dash.

"I don't know how," Mr. Serenity said. "The secrets of this technology died with the fallen. The only way to rescue your brother is to convince Kifo to give up the body."

Ehrich didn't know how he would do this, but he knew that he had to try. He had a new purpose in his life, and, this time, he would not fail his brother.

CATCHING THE TRAIN

Margaret had never wanted to be a hunter. She would have been happy as a sentry or a processing agent, even a gravedigger, but thanks to her excellent marksmanship scores, she found herself on Charlie's squad. She didn't mind the cold nights or the long hours. What the girl hated about the job was the risk. She had already lost Louis to a Dimensional. Now Charlie was fighting for his life in the infirmary because of the traitor, Ehrich Weisz, who seemed to be in league with other Dimensionals. Two years on the squad had made her sick to death of demons. Their filthy bodies had created a permanent reek on Devil's Island. The smell reminded her of the rotting potatoes she'd forced herself to eat when she used to live on the streets.

In the heat of an unseasonably warm autumn afternoon, she detected that scent now. She raised her teslatron rifle at the couple jogging under the Ninth Avenue railroad line. One was the dark-skinned fugitive Commander Farrier had described to the hunters. She wore a pair of magenta goggles over her eyes, an ill-fitting disguise. The figure beside her had his back to Margaret.

"Don't move!" she shouted.

The fugitive's companion spun around—Ehrich Weisz. He grabbed Amina's hand and bolted down the street. Margaret hadn't fully believed Farrier's claim that Ehrich had betrayed Demon Watch, but seeing him run with the fugitive, Margaret now knew he had betrayed his own race. She pressed her cheek against the teslatron rifle as her trigger finger twitched. A horse and carriage rolled through her sightline and she lowered her weapon.

"Amina, keep running!" Ehrich yelled at his bespectacled companion.

They hurried down the street, dodging horse-drawn trolleys and skirting past the pushcart merchants. Ehrich had to vault over a stack of newspapers belonging to one of the newsies on the corner.

A bolt of energy exploded the wall to the right. Ehrich ducked instinctively as he followed Amina through the crowd of screaming nighthawks. They sprinted toward the stairwell, taking two steps at a time until they hit the top.

Margaret waved at Gino and Wilhelm down the street and shouted, "I have the fugitive! Over here! Train platform!"

Ehrich kicked a trashcan down the stairs. This bought them a few seconds at best. Amina scanned the empty platform with her magenta goggles.

"I remember they ran along the tracks," Ehrich said.

"Which direction?"

"That way."

Amina jumped on the tracks and ran north. Ehrich heard a shout and turned. Margaret, Gino, and Wilhelm arrived at the platform. He sprinted after Amina. A shrill whistle blasted the air as a train rounded a corner and rolled straight at the pair.

"Which track were they on?" she yelled as she sprinted along the railroad tracks.

"The one with the train coming at us."

Amina grabbed Ehrich's hand and hauled him toward the oncoming train. He tried to shake himself free, but her grip was too strong. A bolt of energy singed the track to the right. Wilhelm had taken a sniper position on the platform to fire on them. The train whistle blasted again.

"I see it!" Amina yelled.

"See what?!" Ehrich shouted.

The engine chugged toward them, the wheels screeching as the brakes engaged, but there was no way the train would stop in time. Just as Ehrich was about to give himself up for dead, he suddenly felt the tracks give way underneath his feet. All he could feel was Amina's hand grasping his wrist. He floated, untethered from the earth, free from gravity. He saw nothing but an inky void with no end. Just as he was getting used to the weightless feeling, gravity returned with a vengeance and his body plummeted downwards. Light blinded him and pain shot through his legs.

He landed unceremoniously on a smooth jade floor, sprawled out on his back. Amina rolled up, slipping the purple goggles off her head. Red pillars circled a large chamber. Silk sheers festooned floral print walls. At one end of the room, on a raised marble platform, was a canopy bed with mahogany posts and sheer netting. Emerald, bell-shaped lanterns hung from the pillars, bathing the chamber in a soft, green glow.

"Where are we? What happened to the train?" Ehrich asked, completely confused. Had they passed through a portal?

"It's a fold in space," Amina answered.

"What?"

"It's hard to explain. A dimension can be like a shirt. When portals open up, they push the space over, creating folds."

"So it's a portal?"

"No. You can't go through them, but you can go in them and hide from prying eyes. The fold existed in between the tracks of this railroad line. The opening was probably the width of one of the wooden ties across the track."

Ehrich remembered Robert Houdin's memoir and a reference to the Enchanted Portfolio, a thin folder meant only to hold large photographs or artwork. Yet, from the apparatus, the French magician could produce bonnets, birds, and even a boy. The trick was in masking the items' true location and creating the illusion that they were contained in the thin portfolio. This fold in space was Robert Houdin's trick on a grander scale.

"How did you find the fold?" Ehrich asked.

She twirled the goggles by the leather strap. "I had some vision enhancement, but you pointed me in the right direction. Otherwise, it would have been like looking for a strand of hair in tall grass." She stood up and surveyed the room. Her eyes widened and she slowly raised her hands above her head.

Ehrich cocked his head to the side. "What are you doing?"

Amina directed her gaze to the bed. Ehrich turned and saw the barrel of a telescoping derringer emerging through the netting. He raised his hands as well.

A red hand parted the netting to reveal Ning Shu, the crimson-skinned girl from Amina's Kinetoscopic Codex. She stepped off the bed and rose to her full height. Her powerful red leg poked through the slit in her form-fitting *cheong sam.* Scars from countless battles snaked up her bare leg. She held the derringer with a steady hand.

"You've made a fatal mistake," Ning Shu said.

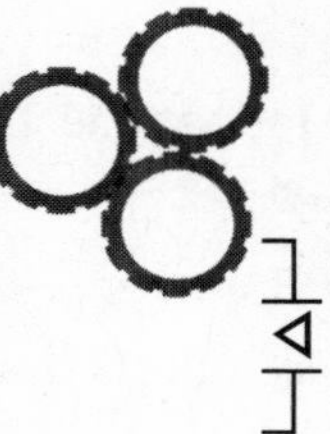

HOUSE OF QI

Ehrich inched back until he was pressed against Amina. He tensed, ready to spring. Behind Ning Shu, a man groaned as he tried to sit up in the bed. He grabbed onto the bed's post, which featured an ornate carving of a dragon spiralling to the canopy. A bandage was wrapped around his neck and his linen shirt was unbuttoned to his stomach, revealing brown stains of dried blood down his hairless chest.

"Who are they, Ning Shu?" he asked.

She flicked her braided queue over her shoulder. "I recognize this one, Hakeem. He's the one who chased us."

"What are you doing here?" the man asked as he stood up.

"Looking for you and her," Amina said. "We were waiting for you at the Museum of Curiosities."

"I don't know you," Ning Shu said.

"My name is Amina. Mr. Serenity sent me. He told me to thank the House of Qi for being a friend to our cause, and to say that your jade tael has an interesting motto."

"A friend of the House of Qi would know the motto. Tell me."

"Death before dishonour."

"Where is Mr. Serenity?" Ning Shu asked. "My deal was with him."

"We'll escort you to him."

"Hakeem is in no condition to travel. Bring Mr. Serenity here."

"Whatever weapon you promised us, we need now. Ba Tian is here in this dimension."

"What? Not possible. My father has no interest in this dimension."

"Demon Gate," Amina said. "A stable portal Ba Tian can use to send his armies through. What weapon do you have against your father?"

"Hakeem," Ning Shu answered. "He was my father's chief engineer. He designed the exoskeleton machines. He knows their weaknesses and can build you better ones—machines that can crush my father's army. But not until you guarantee our safety."

"When we defeat the warlord, everyone will be safe."

"She's right, Ning Shu," Hakeem said. He buttoned his shirt and combed his hand through his thick mane of black hair. In Manhattan, he would have been easily mistaken as one of the Italians in the Bowery, with the exception of his pupils, which were silver. He tried to walk, but lacked the strength. Ning Shu gave him her arm to steady himself.

"What's wrong with him?" Amina asked.

"Someone shot him. It was a small wound and I've stopped the bleeding, but he is weakening with every minute."

Hakeem said. "Every time I exert myself, I feel worse. I think I just need more time to rest."

Ning Shu gently pushed her companion to sit on the bed. He placed his hand on top of hers and gently squeezed it.

"What was the weapon?" Amina asked.

Ehrich answered, "A small dart—shot from a rooftop."

"We kept the dart," Ning Shu said. She picked up the crossbow bolt from the rosewood night table. The projectile was barely longer than her index finger with a sharp needle and hollow cylinder. She handed it to Amina, who sniffed the tip. Her nose wrinkled at the acrid smell but she betrayed no emotion as she turned to Hakeem.

"Have you been running a fever?" Amina asked.

"His forehead burns like a furnace," Ning Shu said.

"Do you have cramps on your right side? Where your appendix is?" she asked as she indicated her abdomen.

He nodded.

"How often does the pain come?"

"Whenever I exert myself. When the pain comes, it feels like I'm being stabbed. When I rest, the pain subsides. I need some rest, then I can meet with Mr. Serenity."

Amina shook her head. "We have something more serious to deal with first."

"What's wrong?" Ehrich asked.

"Hakeem's been poisoned."

Ning Shu shook her head. "No. You're lying. He looks... he looks..." she trailed off.

Hakeem placed his hand to the bandaged wound. "Is the poison fatal?"

Amina sat beside Hakeem and took his pulse. "The dart is

a common design from my world. The preferred weapons of assassins. A chlorotoxin. The poison courses through the system faster when the victim is active. Prevents wounded targets from escaping."

"Is there an antidote?" Ning Shu asked.

"Yes, there is a herb that creates a powerful antitoxin, but it doesn't grow here. I know of another dimension where we can find it, but we have to go now."

"Without a portal, we're not going anywhere," Hakeem said.

Ehrich suggested, "There's Demon Gate."

Ning Shu shook her head. "You said if he exerts himself, the poison will work faster."

"I'll walk slowly," Hakeem said.

"Bring the antidote here. We'll wait," Ning Shu said.

"The only way he has a chance is if we bring him with us. The poison is working its way through his system. Even if he rests, he has a day at most." Amina insisted.

The red-skinned girl refused to budge. "I can't risk moving him."

"You have no choice."

"This is your fault," Ning Shu spat at Ehrich. "Why did you follow us? If you had left us alone, Hakeem would be all right."

"Not true. You were already being stalked. Lucky for you, I was there to see who the shooter was. And now I'm your only way out."

"Can you lead us there?" Amina asked him.

"The only problem is that Commander Farrier has every hunter looking for us both. We can't just waltz in there—but I think I know someone who can sneak us in."

Ning Shu glared at him, then at the pale Hakeem. Her hard

expression faltered as she looked into his eyes, and the pair seemed to come to a silent agreement. Finally, Ning Shu nodded at Ehrich. “Your plan had better work, because if you fail, your head is the first one I’ll take.”

HUNTED

When Ehrich's group emerged from the pocket dimension, the sun was starting to drop below the horizon. He led the trio along the train tracks. Scanning the road below, he spied a patrolling Demon Watch hunter searching low, not high. As long as Ehrich kept everyone to the middle of the railroad line, the hunter wouldn't notice his group. He jogged ahead, scouting for any more patrols. There were none, but he couldn't shake the feeling that they were being watched.

When they were far enough north, Ehrich led them down the stairs of a station and cut across the city toward the pier. Near encounters with hunter patrols slowed their progress. They hid against walls and ducked into yards to avoid detection.

Ehrich pressed forward, moving past an intersection. The scent of the river caught his nostrils. Hakeem seemed to be having trouble catching his breath in the chilly night air.

"Are you all right?" Ning Shu asked.

"Slow and steady and I'll be fine," Hakeem said. He caressed her cheek, but she pulled away when she saw Ehrich watching.

Ehrich pulled Amina aside and whispered, "Are you sure we should have brought him with us? He doesn't look good."

"We might be lucky enough to sneak into Demon Gate, but I doubt very much we'll be lucky enough to come back unnoticed, too."

"Okay, but let's take a rest now," he suggested.

Before she could answer, a voice called out, "I heard something. Over here."

Hunters approached from either direction as Ehrich scanned the narrow street for a place to hide. To the right were a set of stairs leading below street level. Amina ushered Hakeem and Ning Shu down the steps while Ehrich kept an eye on the street.

"They're doing a sweep," he said. "They'll find us soon enough unless I can lead them away."

"We can't risk losing you," Amina said. "You know how to get to Demon Gate."

"They're searching for a lone fugitive. This way I can create a diversion while you get on the boat."

"They're also after me," Amina pointed out.

"You don't know the city. I can lose them in the streets. Wait until the hunters start chasing me, then head to the pier and find a boat. If I'm not back in a few minutes, set off for the smaller island."

"How are you going to get across?" Ning Shu asked.

"I'll get back in time." Ehrich stepped back into the street and walked down the middle of the lane. He approached one of the patrolling hunters and groaned inwardly as he recognized the burly form of Gino, his former squad mate.

Here we go again, Ehrich thought as he charged toward him.

Gino's eyes widened in surprise, and he raised his weapon, but too late. Ehrich jumped through the air and knocked the teslatron rifle out of Gino's hand, sending the hunter to the ground where he slammed the back of his head against the road. He was out cold.

Ehrich grabbed the volt pistol from Gino and shoved it into the back of his pants. Then he took aim with the rifle and fired it at the sky. Shouts of alarm rang out from everywhere, followed by the thump of approaching footsteps. Ehrich fired again to help the hunters locate the source of the teslatron fire.

When the footsteps were close enough, he headed away from the East River, hoping to draw as many of the hunters as he could. Three of them came around the corner. He fired the teslatron at the street near one of them to make sure he had their attention. They returned fire. Yes, indeed, he had their attention. He rounded another corner and headed between rows of brick apartments. Ahead, a fourth hunter appeared: Wilhelm.

Ehrich fired several shots over his head, forcing the teen to take cover. The rifle ran out of energy after the sixth shot. Ehrich tossed the gun aside and sprinted down a side road. He stopped at the door to an apartment building and tried to force his way in but it would not give. He was trapped.

A trio of hunters caught up to Wilhelm as he dragged himself out from behind the thorny hedge. He dusted himself off gingerly and motioned the hunters to follow him.

Crack!

They picked up the pace when they heard the sound of breaking wood. Wilhelm slowed when he reached the side-street. Caution was key. He peeked around the corner. Empty. They raised their weapons and scanned the area. Wilhelm spotted a building to the left and pointed at a door that had been kicked open. He signalled his squad mates to advance.

"Dead or alive, I don't care," he whispered to his squad mates.

He charged through the door. One after the other, the hunters slipped inside the building.

Ehrich peeked up from the bushes across the street and breathed a sigh of relief. Diversion accomplished. He rushed back to the dock to find the others.

A DESPERATE REQUEST

Nikola Tesla hunched over the worktable covered with confiscated items from Dimensionals. Part of his job was to assess them as potential weapons to be incorporated into Commander Farrier's arsenal. Tesla looked forward to this task with grim dread. Most times, the items taken were innocuous trinkets with more sentimental value than military, but an odd item or two sometimes perplexed the scientist. A rare one humbled him. When he discovered these items, he realized how inadequate his knowledge was. Certainly he excelled among the scientists of this world, but compared to some worlds' advanced technologies, he was a child among professionals. He didn't often experience this insecurity, but this evening was one of those times.

He had finally gotten around to looking at the items confiscated from the illegal Dimensional known as Ole Lukoje. The metal glove with sharp talons was of no consequence, but the dust in the man's jacket pockets was astounding. According to Ehrich, the man had used the particles for a variety of purposes, including reanimating the dead. Yet on inspection, even with his magnifying lenses, Tesla could only discern specks. Though baffled by the technology, he refused to call it magic. He never believed in sorcery. To him, the things that science had not explained yet were often passed off as miracles. He had no room in his lab for magic; only for evidence and science.

The only fact he had been able to ascertain was that the dust did not respond well to electricity. He ran a few volts through some of the specks and witnessed a series of mini-explosions. He had to be careful not to set his lab on fire. He swept the remaining dust into a glass jar, hoping someday to solve the mystery.

A noise caught his attention. People were coming up the stairs. He reached for his prototype volt pistol and took aim at the doorway. Ehrich raised his hands.

"Careful, Mr. Tesla."

"Ehrich," Tesla said, lowering his pistol. "I'm most pleased to see you are still alive."

"So far. Why would you think otherwise?"

"Commander Farrier has made some serious accusations. The hunters have been looking for you everywhere. They blame you for injuring a squad leader. They want blood."

"What has Farrier been saying?"

"He claims you helped release Dimensionals from Ninth Circle. He says you are connected to the one who broke into my lab. I had trouble believing the stories."

Amina stepped into the room.

"But when I see this, it makes it harder to deny what I have heard."

Ning Shu carried Hakeem on her back into the lab.

"And harder with every entrance."

"I can explain, Mr. Tesla," Ehrich said. "These are my friends and they are in need of help. They need to use Demon Gate. War is about to break out in New York. A war we can't win without them."

"War? What are you talking about?"

Ehrich brought the scientist up to speed, describing the army he saw amassing in the Hudson River Tunnel Project. He decided to omit the business with Dash and the Infinity Coil for now. Instead, he explained how Hakeem had been poisoned, and how he was the only one who could stop the exoskeleton machines. Tesla observed the younger scientist with keen interest.

"A fellow inventor. I am honoured to have you in my lab."

"I see you are working with polyphase motors," Hakeem said, lowering himself from Ning Shu's back. "Interesting work. The trick is in generating the electromagnetic fields. The brass core can't be magnetized. I would suggest you try something like steel and be mindful of how you position it. Once you can create a harmony between the stator coil and core, you'll reach maximum efficiency."

"I'm impressed. Would you like to see some of my other works in progress?" Tesla asked, thrilled to have another scientist in his presence.

"Thank you, sir, but if you don't mind, I think I need to sit a minute."

Ning Shu helped him to a stool. "Are you all right, Hakeem?"

"Catching my breath. That's all." He smiled at her.

"We can't waste any more time," Ning Shu declared. "We have to get to Demon Gate now."

"She's right," Amina said. "Will your friend help us?"

Ehrich turned to Tesla, "Sir, I wish there was another way to do this without involving you, but you're our only hope."

"There's no way I can sneak all of you in. Every hunter is looking for the two of you," Tesla said, pointing at Ehrich and Amina. "And a Dimensional with red skin? I know people think I'm eccentric, but I doubt they'll believe that I would have her as a lab assistant. No offense," he added with a bow.

Ehrich picked up Ole Lukoje's jacket from the table and draped it over Ning Shu's shoulders. He pulled up the collar, then placed his bowler over her head. The disguise wasn't great, but in dimly lit corridors, the guards might not look twice.

"After all, they're looking for Amina and me," Ehrich said.

Amina tugged at the choker around her neck and said, "Don't worry. I can take care of myself."

"And what about him?" Ning Shu said, pointing at Ehrich.

"I'm not going with you. Mr. Tesla will have an easier time without me, and I can distract the guards. Maybe I'll lead them on a chase around the graveyard."

"Decoy. Clever idea, Ehrich," Tesla said.

"Yes, clever indeed."

Everyone turned to see the Commander Farrier standing behind them, flanked by a half-dozen guards with their weapons raised.

"What did I tell you? Foxes always return to their dens," Farrier drawled.

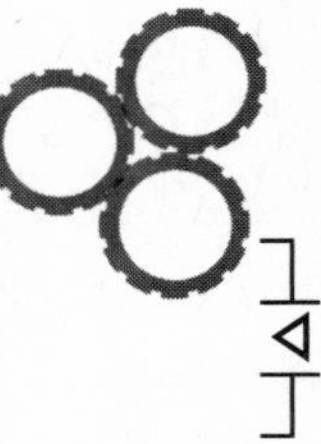

IMPRISONED

Instead of a trip to Demon Gate, Ehrich's ragtag group found themselves taking a one-way trip to Ninth Circle courtesy of Commander Farrier. The guards snapped to attention when they saw the Devil's Island leader limp off the lift. They eyed the new arrivals with glee. Brian, the redheaded Ninth Circle guard, beamed when he saw Ehrich. He ushered everyone onto the funicular platform and personally escorted the group to their cells.

Farrier lingered by Ning Shu's cell as the others were secured in their new lodgings. He whispered to the crimson girl, "I daresay a certain someone will be pleased to know you're safe and in my custody. You'll see him soon enough."

She stiffened. Farrier closed the door in her face, then returned to oversee Ehrich's incarceration. Brian took great delight in frisking Ehrich. He shoved the athletic teen against the wall and was none too gentle about turning out his pockets.

He yanked the boy's dark curly hair to check for any hidden weapons. He even checked inside Ehrich's shoes, before tossing them into the cell. Farrier shoved Ehrich after the shoes, and Brian slammed the door shut.

"Commander, you've convinced the others I'm the enemy, but I know what you are," Ehrich said fiercely. "If they knew what you were up to, they wouldn't be so quick to follow."

"Good soldiers obey orders. Right, Brian?"

"Yes, sir."

"That is a lesson you have yet to learn, Ehrich," Farrier said.

"All those deaths you mourned. The people you lost in the war and now you're about to help start another one."

"This time the right side will win."

"The Dimensionals?" Ehrich asked, aghast.

"No, boy. The South."

Ehrich was dumbfounded. All this time he had assumed when Farrier spoke of the Civil War, he had been fighting for the North. He had no inkling the old commander was a Confederate. What was worse, the peg-legged man had a grudge to settle, and he didn't seem to care how he evened the score.

Tesla stepped into a cell across the corridor and beside the one for Ole Lukoje. The raggedy man waved the stub of his arm at Ehrich and grinned.

"Enjoy your stay," Farrier said. "And stay out of trouble."

The commander limped away with the guards following. Ehrich gripped the bars and gnashed his teeth. If the army of exoskeleton machines in the tunnel was any indication, Farrier and Ba Tian plotted not just a war, but the annihilation of New York and other northern states. He felt powerless to stop them.

He looked down at his shoe and smiled. No, not completely

powerless. He unlatched the fake heel on his right shoe and retrieved the lock pick set. He reached around the bars and tried to manipulate the lock mechanism with his hook pick and tension wrench.

"How does-s-s it feel, fles-s-sh bag, to be one of us-s-s now?" Ole Lukoje taunted.

"Shut up," Ehrich said.

"You have no power over me here. We are now brothers-s-s in mis-s-sery."

Ehrich ignored the illegal and concentrated on picking the lock, but he could sense the raggedy man watching him.

"Excellent job, Ehrich," Tesla called out from the cell next to Ole Lukoje's.

"What's going on?" Amina's voice sounded from down the hall.

"Ehrich is trying to pick the lock of his cell. I'm sure that he will have us free soon enough."

"Hurry," Ning Shu urged. "Your commander told me that my father is on his way here. We shouldn't be here when he arrives."

"We're counting on you, Ehrich," Tesla said.

Ehrich wished the scientist hadn't said that. His hands trembled and he tried to keep the focus on the lock, but he couldn't help looking up at Tesla, who clutched the bars and encouraged him with a nod. He waved at his mentor and smiled, then returned his attention to the lock.

He couldn't tell how much time had passed, but he certainly knew the number of times he failed. Sweat poured down his forehead while insults rained down on his back from Ole Lukoje. Finally, in frustration he smashed his hand against the bars and walked away from the door.

"Take a rest and try again," Tesla advised.

"We don't have much time to waste," Ning Shu called out. "Hakeem needs the antidote."

Ehrich stared at his trembling hands and willed them to stop shaking, but every time he thought about the task at hand, his hands shook even more. He heard footsteps coming toward his cell. He tried to hide his lock pick set, but his hands shook too much to even open the false heel on his shoe.

He turned his back on the door as the footsteps stopped in front of the cell. The sound of shallow rapid breathing came from the other side. Ehrich ran his hand through his dark hair and slowly looked around at Wilhelm.

"What are you doing down here?"

"I heard they brought you in, Houdini," the German boy said. "And I know your tricks. Hand over your shoes."

"Why?"

"Kick them off and hand them over. I know you have something in them. Read it in your magic books."

"Wilhelm, listen to me. I'm not your enemy. The real enemy is amassing an army against New York as we speak."

"Give it up. You're spinning nothing but lies."

"Listen to me, Wilhelm, you have to get off the island and warn someone. An invasion is coming."

"The only enemy I see is the one who betrayed Demon Watch," the husky boy accused.

"Talk to Charlie. He'll tell you."

"He's still in a coma, no thanks to you."

Ehrich swallowed hard. He had hoped his friend's injuries weren't as serious as they seemed. Now he knew otherwise. "Where's he now?"

"Don't pretend you care, Houdini. All the time we spent together as squad meant nothing to you. You care more about these demons than Charlie. You're a traitor."

"Wilhelm, they're not demons. They're trying to help us against Ba Tian."

"Give me your shoes, Houdini."

"Listen to me—"

Wilhelm stood back. "If you make me take them from you, believe me, I'm going to enjoy it."

Ehrich swore and kicked off his shoes. He picked them up and handed them to Wilhelm.

"I'm not the enemy," he said.

"You are a disgrace, Houdini. I always knew something was wrong with you. Now I know why." He sneered as he walked away. "Enjoy your new friends."

As Wilhelm disappeared, Ehrich felt as if he were treading water in an ocean. Just as he had failed Dash, he had failed Charlie. His best friend in this dimension could die because of his actions. Everyone he ever cared about, everyone he loved, was doomed because of his failures.

"Ehrich... Ehrich," Tesla said. "You must not listen to that boy. He is angry. He speaks rashly."

Ehrich ignored him and curled up in a corner of the cell, a ball of abject misery.

"Ehrich?" Tesla whispered. "Are you there?"

He didn't respond.

"Listen to me, Ehrich. You can't blame yourself for what happened to Charlie. You will always wonder—what if you had taken another path? That was the way with me. My brother, Dane. You remember me telling you he died in a horse accident?"

Ehrich looked up slowly.

"Our farm had a path leading to our stables. I was just a child, and I wasn't paying attention to where I was going. I stepped in front of the path. Dane saw me, and he reined the horse into the woods. He rode into a low branch that swept him off, and he struck his head. I ran home to tell my father and mother what had happened, but I left out my role in the accident. Instead, I told them that the horse had been spooked and my brother fell. To this day, I blame myself for Dane's death. But I know my shame cannot be the only thing that defines me, Ehrich. I have moved forward from this. His death is part of who I am, but I cannot let it rule my life. Do you understand?"

Tesla's words were like a rope thrown to a drowning man.

"You can't blame yourself for Charlie," Tesla said.

What Tesla did not—could not—understand, was that Ehrich felt responsible not only for his friend's condition, but also for Dash's current entrapment. He had abandoned the search for his brother in this dimension because he had seen him stabbed in the fight in Five Points. Believing he was responsible for Dash's death, he exiled himself in this world, refusing to go home. He was admitting to himself, finally, that this fruitless quest to find the truth about Dash's medallion had only been an excuse to stay away a little longer, so he wouldn't have to go back to his parents and explain to them how he had lost his little brother. His guilt was paralyzing him.

If only he had continued searching for his brother, he could have saved him, he told himself. If only he hadn't tried to break into Gregor's home to steal back Dash's hat, he might not be here now. If only he had done just one thing differently...

He shook his head to clear it. Those mistakes were in the past.

He had a new responsibility to people in the present. Ba Tian would come to claim Ning Shu and Hakeem, and the only hope Amina and refugees like her had of defeating the warlord would be gone. He didn't know if his actions could stop the war, or revive Charlie, or save his brother Dash, but his inaction would condemn them all. He had to move on. He could change the present, but only if he acted. He walked to the cell door and examined the lock.

Ole Lukoje chuckled. "Are you going to pick the lock with your fingers-s-s?"

Ehrich reached to the side of his head and recovered the hook pick and tension wrench he had hidden in his thick hair. He wiped the tools on his pants. Then he knelt at the door. His hands trembled, but he forced himself to clear his mind. He saw the lock as a puzzle: something he was meant to solve. Something he had practised for late at night in the dormitory when his squad mates were asleep. He inserted the tension wrench and gently pulled the lock mechanism then inserted the hook pick, working methodically, feeling for the delicate click of a pin moving out of its housing. Now that he had cleared his mind, the clicks sounded louder and felt more responsive to his tools. Four clicks later, he opened his cell door.

He grinned at Ole Lukoje as he stepped into the corridor. The creature slunk to the back of his cell, as Ehrich went to work on Tesla's cell. Within moments, all the others were free and gathered in the hallway.

"We have to get Hakeem's antidote," Ning Shu said.

Amina suggested, "Can we get to Demon Gate?"

Tesla shook his head. "Not without a fight."

"We have no weapons," Ehrich added.

Ning Shu held up her jade tael necklace. "Speak for yourself."

"Is that the thing you used when I first met you?" Ehrich asked. "The one that nearly brought the wall down on me?"

Ning Shu nodded. "Looks can be deceiving."

Tesla beamed, repeating his mantra. "Ah, any device can be turned into a weapon, when you are desperate."

Amina shook her head. "It doesn't matter. Any kind of exertion is going to push Hakeem over the edge. Are you okay?"

Hakeem smiled wanly. "I'd feel a lot better if people would stop asking me that question."

Ehrich waved for silence. "Amina is right, we can't use Demon Gate. There has to be another way to open a portal."

A shrill snicker filled the air. They all turned to the source: Ole Lukoje.

He stepped forward. "Life is-s-s rich with irony."

"What are you talking about?" Ehrich asked.

"I am your s-s-salvation," the raggedy man said.

"How? You would have escaped already if you had the means," Ning Shu said.

"She's right," Hakeem said. "The only way to trigger a portal is to use a portal device."

Ehrich agreed. "The guards stripped Ole Lukoje of all his devices. He doesn't have anything that can help us."

Ole Lukoje smiled. "S-s-she does-s-s." He pointed at Ning Shu, who was wearing the raggedy man's jacket.

Her eyes widened. "You're telling me this is your device?"

He shook his head. "Ins-s-side the pockets-s-s."

She reached inside. "There's nothing."

Tesla interrupted, "Are you talking about the dust? I took that out of your pocket. It's in my lab right now. Are those particles your portal device?"

Ole Lukoje nodded.

"Microrobotics," Hakeem guessed. "You're using micro technology."

"What's that?" Ehrich asked.

Hakeem explained, "It is something more advanced than what you have here. My apologies, Mr. Tesla."

"No offense taken. Go on."

"They are miniaturized devices which have the ability to perform many functions. I had experimented with them, but I didn't have the resources to develop them further."

"That's-s-s because-s-se you're from a backward realm," Ole Lukoje said. "And I don't need all the microbots-s-s. Just a s-s-speck or two will do. With s-s-so few I'll need a place that res-s-sonates-s-s with necro energy. Where the dead congregate."

"The graveyard," Ehrich said. "We'd be safe once we got to the surface."

Ning Shu dug into the pocket again and pulled her hand out. She smiled. "It feels like grit on my finger."

Ole Lukoje grinned. "Well, well, well, it looks-s-s like we might have s-s-something to talk about."

Ehrich leaned forward. "What do you want?"

"Wherever you go, I want to go along. I'm tired of my accommodations-s-s. And the food here is-s-s not agreeing with me."

"Set him free," Ning Shu ordered.

"How can we be sure we can trust him?" Ehrich asked.

"It's very simple," she said. She walked to the front of the cell. "My father. Ba Tian. Does that name mean anything to you?"

Ole Lukoje blanched.

"I'll take that as a yes. Ehrich will set you free. When we reach the graveyard, you will open a portal for us. We will go through. Once we are through, your toys are your own again, but if you deviate from my plan, I will show you that I am my father's daughter. Are we clear?"

He nodded. Ehrich almost felt sorry for the raggedy man. Almost.

ESCAPE FROM NINTH CIRCLE

Brian scratched his mop of red hair, wondering how on earth a dog could have slipped into Ninth Circle. The German shepherd had just appeared in the cavern seemingly from out of nowhere. Brian stepped out of the guardhouse along with his five guards. They approached the dog.

Brian clucked, "Come on, boy. Over here."

The dog wagged its tail, and bounded away before anyone could get near. The guards spread out to round up the four-legged intruder.

"Where did the mutt come from?" one guard asked.

"Edwin snuck it down, didn't you? You're the dog lover, aren't you?"

"Yeah, right. I had it under my jacket while you were filling your face with the pork pies I saved for dinner."

They herded the black mutt near the far wall of the cavern. Brian reached out to grab its scruff, but the German shepherd scampered away and bolted for the tunnel leading into the cells.

Brian cried out, "Someone get that dog!"

Four guards lumbered after the animal, chasing it into the tunnel. Brian and another guard headed back to the stationhouse.

"I swear, when I find out who let that dog down here, they are going to be scrubbing cells for the rest of the month," Brian muttered as he walked through the door.

He stopped in his tracks and his mouth dropped open. There, in the stationhouse, stood Ehrich Weisz and Amina holding teslatron rifles. Behind Ehrich, Ning Shu pulled a third rifle from the weapons locker. Ole Lukoje reached out to take it, but she handed it to Hakeem instead as she pulled out another rifle for herself.

"How? What?" Brian sputtered. "You're not supposed to be here!"

Ehrich beamed. "You were always so observant, Brian. Now, drop your weapons and have a seat."

The pair obeyed. Ehrich searched the guardhouse and found some shackles.

Amina scratched her neck where her cameo choker used to be. "How long do you think Mr. Tesla can keep the guards occupied?"

Ehrich shrugged. "Hopefully long enough. Ning Shu, Hakeem, get Ole Lukoje to the lift. Amina, shackle these two."

Ning Shu hoisted Hakeem on her back, then handed him two teslatron rifles to hold as she headed out of the guardhouse behind Ole Lukoje. The trio looked tiny against the vast expanse of the cavern. The lift awaited them behind the jaws of the stalagmites and stalactites. Emerald stalactites hung overhead, catching the light of the lanterns.

In the guardhouse, Amina finished clapping the shackles on Brian and moved on to his female companion.

"You know you won't get away with this," Brian said. "We *will* catch you."

"I've had enough of your voice for one day," Ehrich said. He found a handkerchief on the console, tore it in half, and gagged the two.

Meanwhile, Ning Shu's party had crossed the cavern and climbed into the cage. Ehrich was about to head out of the guardhouse, but he stopped when he noticed Brian's boots.

"What size are your feet?" Ehrich asked.

Brian glared.

"Close enough." Ehrich pulled the boots off the impotent leader's feet and put them on. They weren't perfect, but they fit. "Let's go, Amina!"

They sprinted across the cavern and navigated the jagged stalagmites to get to the lift. Ehrich pulled the lever to activate the mechanism. As the lift rose, he took one last look at Ninth Circle below.

In the cell area, the remaining guards were still running through the corridors, searching for the dog. They swept past prisoners who shook their heads in bewilderment when the guards asked if they had seen a dog run past.

Edwin rested his hands against his knees as he tried to catch his breath. He growled at his comrades. "If word gets out, we're going to be the laughingstock of Devil's Island. No one talks about this. Agreed?"

The others muttered agreement as they split up and searched different corridors. The stocky Edwin lumbered past a row of empty cells, but skidded to a stop. He backed up and looked inside one cell after the other. The only cell that was occupied was the one with Nikola Tesla.

"Where are the others? Ehrich Weisz was right there."

Tesla smiled enigmatically. "Trade secret."

"No. No! No!!" Edwin yelled, running down the hall. "They've escaped!"

Tesla perched on his cot and began to examine Amina's marvellous cameo. The sacrifice he had made to stay behind was a small price to pay.

The lift reached the surface. Ehrich hopped out and motioned everyone to come out. Before they could clear the chamber, the lift began to lurch down the hole of its own accord.

"The guards are on to us," Ehrich said. "We have to stop the lift."

"We don't have the time," Amina argued.

"Disable the mechanism!" Hakeem pointed to the counterweight pulley system over the hole.

Ehrich examined the thick, steel-wrapped cables. There was no way to cut them. Ning Shu lowered Hakeem to the floor and pulled off her jade tael necklace.

"Duck!" she commanded as she whipped the necklace over her head.

She approached the hole and flicked the whining jade tael at the thick cable. The spinning tael sliced through metal like a hand knifing through water. The cable snapped, and the lift plummeted to the depths below. A muffled crash echoed up to them.

Ning Shu fixed a look at Ole Lukoje and said, "See what could happen if you cross me?"

He paled.

She placed the necklace over her head and picked up Hakeem while Ehrich peered down and noted the dust rising up the hole. The cables danced around, unconnected to the lift. Ning Shu had effectively cut off access to and from Ninth Circle.

"Do you have any more of those?" he asked the crimson girl.

She looked at Ole Lukoje. "One is all I need."

Ehrich motioned everyone to head outside. The only light now came from the lamps along the path. He guessed they had been in the prison for a few hours. Farther down the island, the staff dormitories were dark, as were the Demon Watch offices. What Ehrich found odd was the fact that the station guards were absent. He didn't want to take any chances of running into a patrol, so he kept low and close to the iron fence that ringed the graveyard until he reached the entrance. Granite columns bracketed the black gates that Ehrich pushed open. While he swung the gate wide, his companions gawked up at the stone gargoyles atop the pillars.

"What are those?" Amina asked.

"They're guardians."

"They look like they're from s-s-sector 13," Ole Lukoje said. "Nas-s-sty people."

Ehrich motioned them into the graveyard. Ning Shu lowered Hakeem to the ground, took off Ole Lukoje's jacket and handed it to the raggedy man. He reached into the pocket to retrieve his microbots.

"You know what you must do," Ning Shu said.

He nodded, eyeing the deadly jade tael around her neck, before looking back at his hands. "S-s-sad to s-s-see s-s-so few left, but you'll do," he said to them. "Where do you want to go, fles-s-sh bag?"

Amina answered, "Sector 37. The Vena system."

"Ah yes-s-s. A wasteland. No peepers-s-s. You s-s-sure you want to go there?"

"Positive," Ning Shu said.

Hakeem took Ning Shu's hand in his. They shared a look, a silent communication, and she squeezed his hand, her index finger gently caressing his skin for a second.

Ole Lukoje walked to a nearby gravesite. He held his palms up to the sky and released his microbots into the air. Nothing happened. He snatched at the air to collect his gear and moved to the next gravesite to repeat the ritual. Again, nothing. When he tried at the third site, a flicker of tiny light burst in the air, but nothing else.

"There isn't enough necro energy here. I need a recent corpse," he said. "A fresh death would be best. Any volunteers?" He looked at Ehrich with an evil glint in his eyes.

"Follow me," the teen said, ignoring Ole Lukoje's taunt.

He led them through the graveyard toward the graves he had recently dug with his squad. He marched up an incline, but as he reached the crest, he spotted lights in the field and waved everyone back.

The source of the light was coming from a group of about a dozen teens, scurrying across the graveyard. Their bowler hat lamps lit the way as they moved to the eastern side of the island. Among them, a man limped on a peg leg. Commander Farrier. Now Ehrich knew why the guards weren't posted at their stations. Farrier didn't want prying eyes. While Ehrich didn't know where the old man was going, he was pretty sure about who he was going to meet.

Once Farrier's insurgents were far enough away, Ehrich whispered to Amina, "If Ole Lukoje manages to get a portal open before I get back, take everyone through."

"Where are you going?" she asked.

"To make sure you have enough time to get away."

He followed Farrier's rebels to the east shore. A slope led to the rocky beach. The rebels fanned out across the beach with their bowler hat lights on, aimed at the waters. The East River rushed past the island. Bits of flotsam bobbed on the surface, moving swiftly past the shore. Then the water began to glow from underneath. The insurgents murmured to each other, but kept their light focussed on the surface of the water.

A giant iron head emerged from the river. A powerful search beam attached to the forehead shone at the rebels. They stepped back, blinded. The rest of the exoskeleton machine appeared as the contraption stomped toward the shore. Water dripped off the iron limbs as the servos on the joints of the knees and hips powered the massive unit forward. From the light cast by the bowler hats, Ehrich could make out the pilot inside the bubble cockpit—Kifo, in the body of his brother Dash.

[▷] BROTHER VERSUS BROTHER [◁]

Ehrich bit his lip as he watched Kifo wade to the shore. He had to keep reminding himself that the boy was not his brother. Inside the cockpit, the assassin operated levers and pedals to propel the machine forward. Two other exoskeleton units emerged from the water. Ehrich recognized one of the two operators as Ba Tian, the crimson-skinned warlord, and the other as the labourer with the bone-shard mohawk. The servos whirred and spit out water as the machines waded to shore. Air hoses on top of the bucket-shaped heads retracted into their housing units.

Farrier rushed past his insurgents to greet the trio. He shouted over the whirring servos of the exoskeleton machines, "Incredible! I must admit I had some doubts when you promised me war machines. They look impressive, but are they battle ready?"

"Test them if you wish," Ba Tian said, his amplified voice

booming out through the brass horn that blossomed on the top of the helmet.

Farrier waved at a buck-toothed rebel and ordered, "Shoot the one on the left."

The teen raised his teslatron rifle and fired at Kifo's unit. The blast seared the air and struck the exoskeleton unit dead centre. Energy danced across the iron exterior, but didn't phase Kifo who remained safely inside the cockpit. He manipulated a few levers, and the machine lumbered toward the rebel, who backed up and fired another shot. The energy fizzled against its dripping iron hide. Servos powered the massive arm as it reached out and snatched the weapon from the shooter. Kifo pulled another lever and the hand started to crush the weapon, which looked like a child's toy in comparison.

Farrier shouted, "Tarnation! Don't! The teslatron will—"

The gun exploded, knocking the rebels off their feet. The concussion rocked Kifo's unit back three steps, but he remained upright. The light faded as Farrier's group climbed to their feet, now extra wary of the giant machines.

Ba Tian laughed. "Do you need more convincing, Commander?"

Farrier shook a clod of earth off the bottom of his wooden leg and eyed the exoskeleton machine with a soldier's eye. "I don't see any armaments."

Ba Tian raised his giant iron arm and let the weapon turret whir to life. He fired a stream of razor-sharp taels at a willow on the bank. The projectiles sliced through the trunk and the tree toppled to the ground.

Farrier's eyes lit up, but he covered his excitement with a simple nod. "I suppose it will do in a pinch."

"You will have fifty of these units, provided you have enough soldiers to operate them."

The grizzled veteran nodded. "Let me worry about that."

"Now for your end of the bargain. Your messenger said you have my daughter and her companion," Ba Tian said.

"Along with a few others—"

"I'm only interested in my daughter and the traitor. Show me to them."

"Do I look like a newborn colt?" Farrier asked. "When I collect my fifty machines, you can see your family."

"When I see my daughter, we can talk about the transfer."

"No deal, Ba Tian. I want the weapons upfront."

"Tell you what, commander. If we can use Demon Gate, I can deliver one hundred machines instantly."

"That's going to attract too much attention," Farrier said.

The pair went back and forth, bickering about terms and delivery. Ehrich saw all that he needed. He inched away from the shore, but the multitude of voices in his mind began to whisper. They grew louder than ever before.

In the cockpit, Kifo stiffened. He scanned the banks. Ehrich sensed that the assassin was looking for him. The symphony of voices roared. He covered his ears, but the voices were inside his head, begging, pleading, shouting.

Kifo stomped on the pedals and the machine lumbered ahead toward Ehrich's position.

"Where are you doing?" Ba Tian asked, turning from his negotiations.

"My kindred are calling out," Kifo said.

Ehrich's eyes widened. The voices were screaming in his head now. He slipped back from the bank and climbed over the fallen tree just before Kifo reached the top of the slope.

"Running is futile," Kifo called out. Ehrich wasn't sure if he had actually heard the assassin's voice or if it was one of the many echoing in his head.

He headed along the shoreline, leading Kifo away from his friends. The assassin lumbered after him. Lack of speed seemed to be the one weakness of the exoskeleton machine. Farrier motioned for four of his rebels to follow Kifo.

Ehrich raced along the edge of the bank toward the south end of the island, hoping this distraction would buy Ole Lukoje enough time to open the portal. The voices in his head were growing more insistent, distracting him from the presence of a rebel who was cutting up the bank and running toward him. The nimble brown-haired girl tackled him hard to the ground. He rolled and scrambled away, but another insurgent appeared from the bank and drew his volt pistol. Ehrich used his rolling momentum to slam headfirst into the boy's stomach, knocking the wind out of him and sending the gun flying out of his hand. Ehrich then lifted his head straight up and connected with the boy's chin, knocking him out cold. He spun around to see the first girl drawing her pistol as she raced toward him.

He dove for the weapon on the ground as she squeezed the trigger, sending the electro-dart whizzing harmlessly over his head. He grabbed the volt pistol and rolled to the left. A second dart struck the ground just to his right. He fired back. The dart hit the girl in the leg. She shrieked as her entire body lit up, and then collapsed to the ground unconscious.

This encounter had given Kifo enough time to catch up to his quarry. Two of Farrier's insurgents flanked the assassin in the iron contraption. They raised teslatron rifles at Ehrich.

The voices from the Infinity Coil roared in the teen's mind, and he tried to shut them out, but there were too many. He tried focussing on just one voice: Dash's. He sifted through the voices until he could make out his brother's alone, but what he was saying didn't make sense. It was like listening to someone talk through a heavy wall. He could hear the tone of it, but not the substance.

The teen rebels moved ahead of Kifo and approached Ehrich. He recognized the Hill cousins, two southern orphans whose accent was as thick as the cornbread they liked to eat. Ehrich reached into his shirt and pulled out the Infinity Coil. Then he aimed the volt pistol at the medallion. The voices went silent, replaced by Kifo's scream.

"*No*! Unhand my Infinity Coil!" His voice blasted from the megaphone and echoed across the field.

Ehrich shook his head. "You want it, you'll have to come out of that milk churn and get it."

"I've got this," one of the Hill cousins said and raised his teslatron rifle.

Before he could fire, the Hill cousin found himself high in the air, courtesy of Kifo, who held him in his mechanical iron grip. The other Hill cousin was also in the air, screaming for help. The cousins, looking like dolls in the hands of the iron machine, dropped their rifles. Kifo smashed the teens together and knocked them out. Then he tossed their bodies to the ground.

Ehrich backed away until the river water on the southern shore lapped against the heels of his boots. Kifo continued to advance, the machine's heavy feet crushing the rocks underneath.

"One more step and I'll pull the trigger," Ehrich threatened.

Kifo stopped. Ehrich had to remind himself that while the body might be his brother's, the conscience that guided the body was that of an assassin.

"You want this back?"

"It would be unfortunate for you if any harm were to come to my device," Kifo said evenly.

"Let my brother go or I'll destroy it."

"I'll require a replacement," Kifo said.

Ehrich motioned at the unconscious rebels. "Take your pick."

Kifo took another step forward. "You will suffice."

Ehrich's finger twitched on the trigger of the pistol. "I'm warning you—"

The assassin shook his head. "You grasp the consequences if you destroy the Infinity Coil, do you not? You destroy any chance of liberating your brother. Is the reward worth the risk?"

Ehrich didn't give away his doubt. He had to maintain the appearance of calm to pull off this bluff. "I've heard the voices of all your victims. There are hundreds of them. You're an addict looking for a new persona to adopt. You can't just be one person for too long. I imagine that being stuck in my brother's body for two years has been sheer agony. Losing control. Not having the freedom to possess whatever body you want. I don't think you're prepared to give that up."

Kifo took another step forward. "I believe you care about your sibling more. I can hear him within the Infinity Coil. He pines for you. Would you abandon him now in his hour of need?"

The assassin was right. Ehrich had come this far to recover

his brother. He couldn't throw it all away now. His hand began to shake. Kifo smiled and took another step.

"I thought so," Kifo said.

Ehrich couldn't pull the trigger. He willed his finger to squeeze, but it wouldn't budge.

Kifo was almost on top of him.

A chorus of voices shouted inside Ehrich's mind: "*Free us*!"

Kifo stopped. "No, no. Don't."

Ehrich's hand stopped shaking and he looked into his brother's face. He knew what he had to do, and his resolve showed in his expression. He pressed the end of the barrel of the volt pistol into the heart of the Infinity Coil.

"No!" Kifo shrieked. He pushed the pedals of the cockpit, sending it back two steps. Then he unstrapped himself from the cockpit seat and pushed open the glass bubble that housed him. "You wish your brother's return, I will grant it."

"Now," Ehrich ordered.

Kifo hopped down from the exoskeleton's cockpit. "Lower the gun. I'll do as you bid."

Ehrich kept the volt pistol aimed at the Infinity Coil as he followed Kifo up the shore and toward the fallen body of the burly Hill brother. The assassin knelt down and held his hand out for the Infinity Coil. "I will require it to complete the process. Hand me the device."

"One wrong move and I destroy the Infinity Coil. You understand?"

He nodded. Ehrich began to hand over the medallion, but the voices in his head screamed, "*No!*"

Ehrich pulled back but he was too late. Kifo slammed his fist into his gut. Ehrich gasped for air as he tumbled back. He clung to the Infinity Coil's strap as Kifo tried to wrest it away.

The voices in Ehrich's mind exploded into a cacophony of shouts. He shook his head as he struggled with Kifo.

"All of you, silence," Kifo hissed through gritted teeth. Clearly, the voices were yelling in his head as well.

Ehrich punched Kifo in the face. The assassin rolled off. Ehrich tried to climb on top of him, but Kifo brought his knees up and flipped Ehrich over onto his back. The older Weisz brother managed to sit up, but Kifo had already moved in behind him. He grabbed the other end of the tether and yanked the Infinity Coil up so the leather strap hooked around Ehrich's neck. He gasped for air as the strap slipped tighter and tighter. Ehrich smelled sulphur and, for an instant, he felt himself separating from his body. The voices sounded like they were next to him now. Was he passing out, or was he being absorbed into the Infinity Coil? He couldn't tell.

Suddenly, he saw Dash in front of him. Not the cold-eyed boy who had been possessed, but the fresh-faced kid who had looked up to his big brother. They were no longer on the shore of Devil's Island. Instead, they were floating in a sort of limbo. Ehrich reached out to touch his brother's arm, but his hand passed through. He looked at his own hand and saw through it as if it were translucent. Where was he?

Dash yelled, "Fight!"

Suddenly, Ehrich opened his eyes and saw the East River ahead. He felt the hard rocks under his legs. He noticed his volt pistol a few feet away. He heard the gears clicking on the Infinity Coil. Without another second's hesitation, he slammed himself backward, knocking the back of his head against the nose of the assassin. The strap loosened, giving Ehrich a chance to take another breath as he slammed himself back again. Kifo grunted, but didn't let go.

Ehrich swung his elbow around hard. He caught Kifo in the ribs and knocked him sideways. Then he angled his head so that the noose slipped off. He saw the Infinity Coil glowing in the assassin's hand just before he shoved Kifo into the river. Ehrich crawled across the rocks to retrieve his fallen volt pistol. Kifo rose up in the water, holding the Infinity Coil by the leather strap.

"Finally!" Kifo roared.

Ehrich raised the pistol and fired the electro-dart into the assassin's chest. Electricity lit up his body and arced to the Infinity Coil. Kifo fell backwards into the water as the sizzle of energy filled the air, but all Ehrich could hear was the anguished cries of hundreds of voices in his mind. Then all was silence.

He raced into the river and searched the waters. He swept his arms under the surface, trying to grab his brother's body. There was nothing but cold murky water. Desperately, Ehrich waded farther from the shore. He called out in his mind, "Dash, where are you? Dash!"

No response. It was as if the voices within the Infinity Coil had been snuffed out.

DEVIL'S ISLAND BESIEGED

Ole Lukoje hopped from one foot to another as a sliver of a dimensional portal appeared. "It's-s-s working, but I need more necro energy," he said.

"Keep at it," Amina ordered.

She focussed her attention back onto the approaching enemy: two exoskeletons and a group of Farrier's rebels. Amina had two options. She could run or fight. The promise of the gateway was too tempting.

She turned to Ning Shu and Hakeem. "We have to give Ole Lukoje more time to open the portal. It's Hakeem's only chance."

The scientist wiped sweat from his brow. He was pale and weak, but he gripped his teslatron rifle and said, "No other choice."

Ning Shu lay down and took aim with her rifle. "Amina, your highest priority is Hakeem."

Amina nodded. She lay flat on the ground a few paces away

from Hakeem, who aimed his teslatron rifle at the advancing pair of exoskeleton machines.

Hakeem instructed her, "Aim at the servos. That's the weak point of the units. It won't stop them, but it will slow them down if we can score a direct hit."

She nodded and inched away from him. Ba Tian's machine suddenly raised its arm with the weapon turret. The carousel began to spin and whine until a high-pitched scream filled the air.

"He sees us," Ning Shu said as she stood up in between them. "Stay behind me."

"Ning Shu, are you crazy? Get down!" Amina ordered.

The red girl whipped off her jade tael and whirled the necklace until the air vibrated with the hum of the device. Ba Tian unleashed razor taels at the trio. They pinged off the whirling shield Ning Shu had created with her jade tael. Amina and Hakeem fired on the approaching machines.

Suddenly, Farrier's insurgents appeared from behind the units. They spread out across the graveyard and returned fire. The night sky was illuminated by the teslatron bolts hammering Ning Shu's shield. Amina shot at the exoskeleton nearest her. The shot lit up the exoskeleton unit, but missed the servos.

On the other side of Ning Shu, Hakeem inched himself to the edge of her spinning shield and fired at the stray insurgents trying to flank them. He was a scientist, not a warrior, and his shots went wide and high. Ba Tian and his fellow exoskeleton operator advanced on their position. Their only hope now was Ole Lukoje.

"I don't care what you have to do to open the portal, but do it now!" Amina yelled.

"Patienc-c-ce," the raggedy man answered.

Amina spotted four of Farrier's insurgents flanking past Hakeem's defenses. She swung her rifle around and shot at the rebels. One went down. The rest took cover behind the grave markers. Amina pinned them down so that she could protect Ole Lukoje as he worked on the portal. She advanced on the rebels, leaving Hakeem and Ning Shu to hold off the machines and the rest of Farrier's insurgents.

Ning Shu shouted at Hakeem, "The humans are moving on the right. Take them down."

Hakeem crawled to Amina's former position on Ning Shu's right. He fired at two insurgents moving through the grave markers. His bolt seared a wooden cross, but missed the pair completely. He coughed as he tried to reposition for another shot.

"Hakeem, are you all right?" Ning Shu asked.

"Stop asking!" he snapped.

Before Ning Shu could check on him, a round of razor taels pinged off her shield. Her arm burned in pain from twirling the jade tael. The two exoskeleton machines moved closer. She couldn't keep this up for much longer.

Then, from the right, a hail of projectiles slammed into one of the machines. A few more jammed into the metal hide. They were razor taels. She looked to the right and saw a third exoskeleton unit lumbering erratically across the graveyard. The operator hadn't fully mastered the controls, but seemed to know how the weapon turret worked at least.

Ehrich smiled grimly from the cockpit.

He had figured out that the pedals operated the legs, and he pumped them to make the unit move forward. The levers in front of him controlled the arms, and he had found the lever that operated the turret. He pulled on it again to send a fresh volley of razor taels at the attackers.

The taels cut down the grave markers and bit into a trio of rebels that were moving toward Hakeem. They dropped their weapons and fell to the ground, bloodied and screaming in pain. Ehrich could hear all the sounds of the battle through the cockpit's interior brass horn, a mini-version of the one attached to the outside of the helmet.

Farrier fired his teslatron rifle at Ehrich while he barked at the remaining insurgents around him. "Charge that machine!"

They obeyed. An amazon of a girl fired her weapon and scored a direct hit on the cockpit. The energy dissipated against the non-conductive material, but Ehrich still flinched instinctively. He pulled another lever and the weapon turret swung to the left, then to the right. He fired as the arm swept across the field. The insurgents dropped to the ground for cover. He tried to bring the arm around to aim low at the rebels.

Before Ehrich could fire, the amazon girl stood up and shot her teslatron. The others moved in behind her and charged at Ehrich while unleashing volleys of energy bolts at his machine. Farrier let loose a rebel yell that sounded like a cross between a whoop and a wolf howl. Ehrich's skin crawled from the sound of it. He yanked on the lever and fired the turret again. The taels cut into the legs of his attackers, mowing them down. They screamed as they collapsed to the ground. Farrier called out to his new ally.

"Ba Tian!" the old man cried. "They've taken one of your machines!"

But the warlord was too intent on wiping out his daughter's shield.

The commander banged on the back of the unit's iron leg to no avail. He limped away to join the rebels engaged in battle with Amina. She fired at him, but an insurgent dove in front and took the blast. Farrier limped to safety behind the remaining two rebels.

Another roar of the turret filled the air, deafening Amina. She glanced over at where Ba Tian and his soldier were firing at Ning Shu's shield. They were closing in the gap and were almost on top of her.

Ba Tian shouted through the cockpit, "You choose the traitor over your own flesh and blood?"

"You never learned when enough was enough, father. Your greed is your greatest weakness."

"I don't care if you're my daughter. No one betrays the House of Qi." He yelled to his exoskeleton comrade, "Leave her to me! Take out the traitor!"

The bone-shard mohawk operator nodded and his iron machine lumbered toward Hakeem.

Ning Shu cried out, "Hakeem, come to me. Walk. Crawl. I don't care. Just get here!"

He struggled to move, but he was too weak and could barely crawl a foot. Ning Shu inched toward him, but her father's machine unleashed a fresh volley of taels, forcing her to hold her position and maintain her shield. Hakeem crawled toward Ning Shu as the other exoskeleton unit flanked the crimson girl.

Ehrich wrenched the levers to spin his machine ahead to take down the other exoskeleton. He pumped the pedals and drove his unit to confront the deadly attacker, but he was running out of time. When he tried to position the turret to fire, the lever jammed. The arm wouldn't lift. He struggled with the controls, but they would not budge.

The other exoskeleton's weapon turret was levelled at Hakeem. The scientist leaned against a marker with the rifle across his lap. His head slumped to one side.

"Hakeem!" Ehrich yelled. "Fire on him. Hakeem!"

The scientist didn't budge.

Ehrich yanked on the lever one more time, and finally the arm responded. A stream of taels flew into the servos of the exoskeleton. Sparks flew, and the air filled with the screech of metal on metal. Ehrich fired again. Taels struck the servos on the machine's right side until something twanged. The contraption listed to one side and toppled over. The machine hit the ground face first, pinning the operator underneath. Ehrich pulled the lever again, but the turret was out of ammunition.

A flash of light caught Ehrich's attention as the portal suddenly widened. Ole Lukoje yelled, "It's-s open! It's-s open!"

Amina ordered, "Get Hakeem and take him through. I'll cover you."

Ole Lukoje hesitated, eyeing the escape, and took a step toward the gateway.

She raised the rifle at him. "Don't even think about running out on us."

He backed away from the portal and skittered across the graveyard to Hakeem.

"Ning Shu, the portal's open!" Amina cried out.

The crimson girl called back, "Get Hakeem out. I'll make sure my father doesn't follow." She advanced on her father's machine with her jade tael spinning at full speed. Ba Tian roared as he unleashed a volley of razor taels at the shield, but then his turret ran out of ammunition. Father and daughter were at a standoff.

Amina backed up to the portal as she fired on the flanking rebels. She took down the last two as she reached the gateway. Through the portal, she saw red skies stretching over the devastation, and blackened ground from the war that had ravaged this world. Her heart filled with grief at the sight. An energy bolt struck her in the arm. Pain lit up all her senses as she dropped her rifle and fell to the ground. Farrier beamed as he stood up from his hiding spot behind a grave marker.

"Ole Lukoje, hurry," Amina gasped as she struggled to stay conscious.

The raggedy man reached the scientist. "Your s-s-salvation is-s-s at hand."

Hakeem didn't respond.

"No time to res-s-st your peepers-s-s," Ole Lukoje said.

Silence. The man's eyes were open, staring blankly at the sky. He was gone.

"Fles-s-h bag? Hakeem!" Ole Lukoje said, nudging his arm.

Ning Shu saw Hakeem's body slump to the ground. "Hakeem!"

She released her jade tael necklace. It flew high in the air and fell to ground many grave markers away.

"No, no, no. Hakeem. Please. Not now," Ning Shu cried, as

she embraced the scientist's still form.

Ba Tian stomped closer to his daughter. He loomed over her. Ole Lukoje backed away from the giant machine, his nose whistling loudly.

"Get out of there, Ning Shu!" Amina gasped.

The girl refused to budge.

"You betrayed me for love?" Ba Tian bellowed. "Have you learned nothing from me? Love is a weakness that your enemies will exploit."

She spat at her father, "I don't care what you think. Finish the job and let me join Hakeem in death."

Ba Tian pulled on the levers to lift his unit's iron arms above Ning Shu's head. She refused to step aside or defend herself.

Ehrich stomped down on the pedals to propel his unit forward, and he manipulated the levers to lift the iron arms up. With a resounding crash, his machine collided with Ba Tian's exoskeleton unit.

The cockpits were face to face. Ba Tian roared in anger as Ehrich powered his exoskeleton machine to drive his opponent back. But in this particular technology, Ba Tian was a seasoned warrior. The massive iron hands slammed into Ehrich's cockpit, crushing the unit and pressing the sides against his body as the shield exploded in his face.

He pumped the pedals and drove Ba Tian's machine away from Ning Shu and toward the portal. The warlord's unit drove its iron fists into Ehrich's cockpit again. The harness straps of his seat dug into his shoulders as the cockpit bent out of shape. He pushed a lever and lifted his iron arm up, catching Ba Tian's machine under the armpit. The stick locked up, but Ehrich put both hands on it and pushed until the other unit lifted off the ground. Ehrich pumped the pedals and marched closer to the portal.

Ba Tian powered his iron arm to smash a fist on Ehrich's cockpit again. The iron hand began to come down on the teen's head. Ehrich closed his eyes and gave the lever one more push. The massive iron arm lifted the other exoskeleton unit high in the air just as the iron fist swung down. The weight shifted and Ehrich's unit toppled over face first. He pulled on the lever and released Ba Tian's machine. The teen felt his nose break as it connected with the ground. He was pinned in the cockpit and trapped under the massive unit.

He angled his head to watch what was going on. Out of the corner of his eye, he spotted a figure dart across the graveyard. He saw Ning Shu sobbing over Hakeem. Then he smiled as he saw Ba Tian's machine fall through the portal and land on the other side.

"Ning Shu, close the portal! Use the rifle. Fire it at the gateway."

She didn't respond.

"Take revenge on your father and fire at the portal!" Ehrich cried out.

That order spurred Ning Shu into action. The crimson girl searched the ground for a weapon and spotted Hakeem's rifle. She stooped down to pick it up, but an energy bolt seared her back. Electrical energy danced up and down her emerald robe as her body arched backwards. She collapsed, her body smoking from the shot that came from George Farrier. He now took aim at Ehrich.

Before the commander could pull the trigger, an energy bolt sizzled over his head, missing him by inches. He scanned the area and saw Amina repositioning her rifle to get a better shot at him. Knowing the value of retreat, Farrier backed out of the graveyard. Amina kept firing the rifle, but her injured arm prevented her from getting a good aim. Once the weapon fizzled, drained of its charge, she began to crawl doggedly across the ground to the rifle Ning Shu had set down.

Meanwhile, Ehrich was trapped in the cockpit of the exoskeleton war machine. He tried to free himself, but the buckles on the harness straps wouldn't release. They essentially held Ehrich in an iron coffin.

He angled his head to the other side and spotted Ole Lukoje standing up.

"Shoot the portal before Ba Tian comes back through!"

Something was wrong with the raggedy man. His eyes were glazed over. Suddenly his body arched. The overpowering smell of sulphur filled the air. The raggedy man's face distorted. He staggered forward, his eyes wide with fear. He mouthed, "Help me."

Then his body went limp and he fell to the ground. Behind him stood Kifo, holding the Infinity Coil. The gears whirled and clicked. Ehrich yelled, "Kifo! Let my brother go!"

The assassin grinned, "I appreciate my kindred exactly where they are."

The Infinity Coil made one final click, and Kifo's eyes rolled to the back of his head. His body, which once held the assassin, was now an empty shell. Like a puppet whose strings had been cut, the body collapsed.

Ehrich tried to free himself from the cockpit, but he was wedged in.

"No!" he shouted.

The body of Ole Lukoje no longer belonged to the raggedy

man. The one who was now climbing to his knees was its new owner, Kifo. He examined the stub of his amputated arm and whistled as he breathed. "A broken body, but this-s one has-s other talents-s-s."

Amina struggled to reach for the teslatron rifle.

Kifo smiled. "No, I don't think s-so." He hopped toward Amina. He kicked the rifle out of her reach. It slid across the grass and stopped a few feet away from Ehrich. The assassin towered over her.

"No!" Ehrich yelled as he looked at the portal.

The iron hand of Ba Tian's exoskeleton machine emerged through the gateway. Ehrich struggled with the harness, but he was trapped.

Kifo straddled Amina and began to choke her. She tried to kick him off, but she was too weak. "Help," she gasped.

Another iron hand emerged through the portal. Ba Tian was coming back into the dimension.

"Get off!" Amina screamed and kicked at the assassin, but she had little energy left. He cocked his head to one side, examining her eyes.

Ehrich squirmed to escape from the cockpit harness. Then he forced himself to relax. He took a deep breath, then arched his back and squeezed in his stomach as he contorted himself out. He was able to lower his right shoulder enough to slip it out, then he raised his arm and slipped the other harness strap off the left shoulder. The jagged edges of the cockpit shield cut into the palms of his hand as he gripped the sides and hauled himself free. But his leg was caught. He kicked, but he couldn't slip out of the twisted harness.

Ba Tian's cockpit was now visible. Ehrich kicked his leg once more to shake off the leather restraints and reached out to grab the teslatron that was inches away, but he couldn't get it.

"I have no idea why, but your orbs-s look delectable," Kifo said as he squeezed Amina's delicate throat.

Ehrich gave in to the harness and let his foot relax as he pushed it down. The strap went slack and he slipped his foot out. He crawled out from under the unit and stretched across the ground to grab the rifle. He turned it on Kifo, but stopped when he saw Ba Tian's machine emerge fully from the portal.

That moment, Tesla's words rang in his ears: "Any device can be turned into a weapon, when you are desperate." He had one shot at this, and he couldn't waste it.

He hurled the rifle directly under the iron foot of Ba Tian's machine as it was coming down. Ba Tian's iron foot stepped on the teslatron and the weight crushed the gun.

An explosion rocked the ground. Ehrich's ears rang from the blast, and he had to blink away the bright light. The concussive force drove Ba Tian back into the other dimension, and the branches of electricity that flew off the rifle lit up the gateway, causing it to close in on itself. In an instant, the portal was gone and so was Ba Tian.

Ehrich glanced over to Amina. She was prone on the ground. There was no sign of the assassin. Ehrich scanned the grave markers—the explosion must have knocked Kifo off his friend. A few feet away lay Ning Shu and Hakeem. He started crawling toward them, but he then he spotted the body of his brother. The two years they had been apart now felt like a speck of time. He crawled to his brother's still form, picked up the limp boy, and cradled his head in his arms.

"Dash," he croaked. "Wake up. It's me. Ehrich."

No answer. Ehrich passed his hand under his brother's nose and felt a waft of air. He was alive. Ehrich scanned the graveyard for Kifo, but he was gone. Ehrich closed his eyes and tried to listen for his brother's voice. Nothing.

OCTOBER 23, 1890 *NEW YORK WORLD*

DEMON GATE UNDER ATTACK

New York, Oct. 23 – Authorities are still investigating the incident that occurred on Devil's Island three nights ago. It is believed that Dimensionals attacked Demon Gate, the facility tasked with processing new immigrants from other realms.

The identity of the instigators is currently unknown, but authorities have discovered evidence of advanced weapons technology employed in the attack. Twelve Devil's Island guards were seriously injured. Commander George Farrier is missing and presumed dead.

This incident marks the first ever assault on the facility that keeps New York safe from the Dimensionals. The mayor has called for a full review of Demon Gate and has appointed Thomas Edison as commissioner to oversee the investigation.

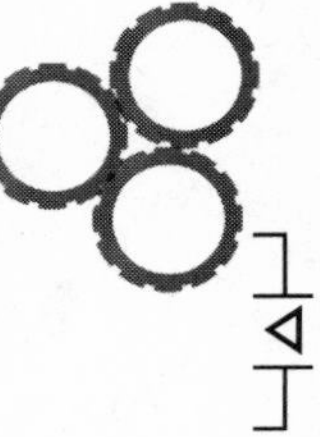

HOPE RISES

"Stare at the newspaper any longer and your eyes are going to fall out," Mr. Serenity quipped.

Ehrich looked up. "Don't you think it's curious the article doesn't mention Mr. Tesla? By now someone must have made their way down to Ninth Circle. Do you think he's all right?"

"If he's half the man you described, I'm sure he's having a grand old time with Amina's device." Mr. Serenity set plates and utensils on the table.

"With Thomas Edison in charge, I'm sure Mr. Tesla is in for a miserable time."

"Then maybe your friend needs a break from Devil's Island," Mr. Serenity said.

"They'll have guards watching him 'round the clock."

"Nothing is impossible," Mr. Serenity said, smiling enigmatically. "Now, help me set three more chairs around the table."

The teen stood, folding his newspaper and tucking it under his arm as he grabbed a chair to add to the two already at the table. Mr. Serenity added two more, bringing the total to five.

Amina entered, carrying two steaming bowls. One was filled with golden yellow corn kernels; the other had purple broccoli-like florets bobbing in an aromatic brown broth. She set them both on the table then gestured to Ehrich and Mr. Serenity. "Sit, please."

As Ehrich took his seat, he asked, "So, what's this?"

Amina stirred the corn with a wooden spoon. "This is mahindaize. Like the corn of your dimension—only sweeter. And this dish is hzintalli. The closest dish would be what you call stew. Hzintalli translates to hearty and filling."

"What's the occasion?" Ehrich asked.

"We stopped Ba Tian from destroying another dimension. I think this is cause enough for a shared meal," Mr. Serenity said.

"We?" Amina said, raising an eyebrow at her mentor.

"You did the heavy lifting, but I was there in spirit."

She rolled her eyes and left the room.

Ehrich nodded to the fifth empty chair and asked, "Mr. Serenity, who else is joining us?"

"Ning Shu."

"That makes four. Who is the fifth chair for? Wait. Did you have any success with Dash?"

He shook his head as he rested his elbows on the table's smooth black surface. "Sorry, Ehrich. Your brother is still in the cryogenic incubator."

Ehrich pictured his brother looking serene in the glass sarcophagus, where Mr. Serenity had hooked a cable to a generator which chilled Dash's body to freezing temperatures and temporarily suspended his bodily functions.

"Son, you do understand there's only one cure for his condition," Mr. Serenity said. "We must find Kifo and—"

"I know, I know," Ehrich interjected. "We have to convince him to release Dash from the Infinity Coil."

"And I don't think Kifo will be amenable to our request."

Ehrich would rather face those insurmountable odds than give up on his brother again. His guilt was a scab on his conscience, healing slowly, but only if he didn't pick at it. As his mentor Tesla had advised, he could let the past inform who he was, but he couldn't let his guilt dictate his life. If he failed to save his brother, it would not be from lack of effort. "You said it yourself, Mr. Serenity. Nothing is impossible."

The stout man clapped his meaty hand on Ehrich's shoulder. "Bravo. I like your spirit, son."

"So, who is our fifth guest, sir?"

"Ning Shu asked for a fifth place, that's all she said."

Amina returned, carrying a dish covered with a white tea towel. Behind her, Ning Shu cradled a mask—Hakeem's face cast in burnished copper. The contours of the metal mask had been moulded properly to match Hakeem's high cheekbones and wide forehead, but the details of the arch of his eyebrows and the mole on the side of his nose were handcrafted with painstaking care by someone who knew his face intimately. Ning Shu gently placed the death mask on the table in front of the empty chair. The fifth guest had arrived.

Amina cleared her throat to get everyone's attention. "My mother used to say that sharing a meal reminds us life is a journey we take together, no matter where we are from. Mahindaize was the major crop in my world. Mahindaize sustained my people.

Hzintalli is a stew made from what survived the invasion."

"It reminds us that life perseveres," Mr. Serenity added.

"Yes." She offered the bowl of corn to Ning Shu, who nodded and dished a spoon of the warm kernels on her plate. Then she dished some onto a plate for Hakeem's death mask, before passing the bowl to Ehrich, who raised an eyebrow, confused.

Ning Shu explained: "To ease Hakeem's transition to the eternal sleep, his death mask experiences part of Hakeem's life."

"An exquisite design," Mr. Serenity said. "How did you learn to do this?"

"From my father. We fashioned the death mask for my mother. It was the first time in a while that we were together for longer than a meal. For two days we did nothing but study her face—her lines, her hair, even her freckles. Then, when we were ready, my father mixed the compounds and cast her face in the bronze mould. He said the cast could only capture the shape of my mother's face; we had to breathe our memories into her features. He guided my hand when I carved the worry lines along the bronze forehead and he told me stories. How they shared their first kiss under the mulberry tree that grew outside my bedroom window. How, when my grandmother died, I couldn't stop crying until Mother wrapped her arms around me. My father said he stood outside the room, watching, unwilling to come in. He said this was a cherished moment between mother and daughter, and he knew better than to interrupt. He told me the stories would ease my mother's transition from life to death." Ning Shu's face contorted into a grimace of pain. "He wouldn't shed a tear for my mother—claimed the death mask was a celebration of her life, but I knew he was lying. When he thought he was alone, he caressed her cheek. He looked so lonely and lost without her. I watched from behind a pillar as he leaned over and kissed her bronze lips. I wanted to hug him, but I knew this was his moment. His story to her.

"When Hakeem came to me with his doubts about continuing to work for my father, I told him he had to quit and leave. He was so scared of my father that he refused to even entertain the idea of defecting. I told him this story of my father to show him that Ba Tian, the cruel and merciless warlord of the House of Qi, could be as lost and vulnerable as any man. And if he feels pain like any man, he can be defeated. Hakeem's death opened the portal and allowed us to banish my father. This is the story I give to his death mask to take to the other side."

"I wish I knew him so I could give him a story," Ehrich said.

"You can share a meal with him and remind him life continues," Ning Shu said. "This looks incredible, Amina."

"Thank you. Everyone please eat. Let's give Hakeem a proper send off."

Mr. Serenity spooned the hzintalli into his mouth and his face puckered as if he had sucked a lemon. Ehrich followed suit and nearly gagged on the sour milk taste swilling around his tongue.

"Is something wrong?" Amina asked.

"The path to your destiny does not go past the kitchen," he said.

"Can't be that bad," Ning Shu said. She took a bite and self-consciously chewed for several minutes until she could force down the food. "The meat...has a...a...robust texture."

"I don't care what any of you say, this is the food of my people and I will not be insulted." Amina scooped a healthy portion of both hzintalli and mahindaize into her mouth, chewed once and delicately regurgitated the mixture on to her plate.

Everyone burst into laughter. Ehrich pushed his dish toward Hakeem's death mask. "We shouldn't be the only ones to suffer."

More laughter.

"Okay, okay. From now on, I'll stick to the battlefield," Amina proclaimed.

"Our stomachs thank you," Mr. Serenity quipped. "I think I have a Xibanic loaf in the pantry."

He left the room.

Ehrich leaned back in his chair. "So now that Ba Tian is gone what happens to his army?"

Ning Shu answered, "They are soldiers. Trained to follow orders."

Amina added, "And if Kifo is in league with your father, I suspect he will have orders for them."

The red-skinned girl nodded. "It will only be a matter of time before my father finds a portal back here. We've delayed his plans, but we have not stopped the war."

Silence filled the room as the weight of the truth settled on the trio.

Amina straightened up. "Ning Shu, you said the soldiers will follow orders, right?"

She nodded.

"If Ba Tian and Kifo aren't there, who would they follow?"

"The one who bears the symbol of the House of Qi," Ning Shu said, holding up her jade tael.

Amina asked, "And other than your father and Kifo, who knows that you have defected?"

"No one. My father wouldn't be able to stand the shame of his own daughter turning against him. It would make him look weak."

Ehrich cracked a smile. "Amina, you're talking about a magic act. With Ba Tian missing, the rightful heir would take his place and lead the army, and that's Ning Shu. By the time Ba Tian comes back, we'll have control of his war machines."

"Where does the magic come in?" Ning Shu asked.

"We have to make Kifo disappear," Ehrich said.

Smiles broke out across the table. They were united in cause and mission. Mr. Serenity returned to the room empty handed.

"Apologies. I thought I had Xibanic, but I couldn't find anything."

"That's okay," Ehrich said. "What about the covered dish?"

Amina lunged and grabbed the dish. "I don't think I can stand any more of your comments about my cooking."

Ehrich pleaded, "Let's just take a look."

"Yes, maybe you lucked out on this one," Mr. Serenity said, chortling.

Ning Shu admonished him. "We've mocked her enough. Amina, if we promise not to tease, will you show us what you've made?"

"Do you swear?" Amina asked, fixing her gaze at Mr. Serenity.

"Buttoning my lip. Nothing comes out, nothing goes in. Sorry, last one."

Amina picked up one end of the tea towel. "I made this for you, Ehrich," she said as she lifted the towel off to reveal a pie with a golden brown crust.

Ehrich beamed. "Apple?"

She nodded.

“How did you learn how to bake an apple pie?” he asked.

“I had to ask around Purgatory until I found someone who worked for a baker above ground. He gave me the ingredients and instructions. I hope the pie is right.”

“Only one way to find out,” Ning Shu proclaimed, grabbing a knife and cutting pieces for everyone.

“You didn’t have to do this,” Ehrich told Amina.

She smiled. “Everyone needs a little something from home.”

“Well, thank you,” he said, taking a bite of the pastry. It was a surprisingly big-hearted but completely inedible piece of apple pie.

“Well?” Amina asked. “What do you think?”

Ehrich smiled as his new friends looked at him expectantly. “Tastes like home.”

INFINITY COIL

The adventure continues
FALL 2014